HALF PAST PECULIAR

FINDERS CREEPERS

DEREK FRIDOLFS AND **DUSTIN NGUYEN**

Scholastic Inc.

For Maximus. A loyal companion.
A fighter until the end. And greatly missed.
—Derek

For Bradley and Kaeli. Stay inspired and seek adventure every day.
—Dustin

THE HOLLOW HERALD

TOWN HALL RECORDS

The city of THORNS HOLLOW was founded in the year 1642 by frontiers-woman ABIGAIL CROWLSLEY. Not content to live in the earliest colonies of settlers on the east coast of the Americas, headstrong and earnest Abigail struck out toward the northwest on her sixteenth birthday with only her loyal Irish Setter as her traveling and hunting companion. After surviving a harsh winter living off of snow birds and berries, she settled in an unclaimed valley. This unique area was noted for having one perpetual season of autumn. The valley's dreary fading colors, falling leaves, and dying trees became the town of Thorns Hollow. And because of its sleepy qualities, it has also become home to one of the largest populations of domesticated animals as its residents attempt to combat the dourness.

CHAPTER 1

In the middle of the city, in the middle of their neighborhood, was a house that everyone knew.

Their father was a deep-sea explorer. Their mother, a relic hunter and professor. And the children were twin siblings who followed in the family business of searching for things.

This was the home of the family Fetch.

At the edge of the lawn stood a metal mailbox, shaped in the form of a dog. With one quick twist of its metal tail, it released its mouth hinge, allowing the stack of letters to be retrieved by a girl, who ran up the sidewalk to burst through the front door.

"Mail call!" Esmeralda yelled, chucking the letters onto the kitchen table.

"Let's see what we've got," answered Atticus, entering the room to greet his sister.

The Fetch Twins were of normal size and stature for children their age. Esmeralda was half a head taller and seventy-four seconds older than her shorter and younger brother. Both had dark hair. Both a thin frame. While Atticus was the more book smart of the two, Esmeralda was the more adventurous, with bruised knees and elbows to prove it.

But they both had one thing in common: a desire to find missing pets.

Atticus flipped through the stack of mail, carefully separating it into piles, before arriving at the most important piece. "Bills, advertisements, and a card."

"From who?" asked Esmeralda, already eating a banana she took from the fridge.

"Jack Webster. Thanking us for finding his dog, Disco."

"Pretty clever of you adjusting the fire sirens to amplify a melody while driving around town. That dog is drawn to music," smirked Esmeralda. "How did you get the fire department to agree to that?"

"Well, they did owe us a favor for finding their firehouse dog, Spot, the week before," replied Atticus.

Esmeralda quietly walked over and stood behind her brother. Only after reading through the rest of the mail did he realize she was there, waiting to be noticed.

"Okay, what is it? Is there something else?" asked Atticus, almost afraid to find out. "And please don't muss up my hair."

"Only this," said Esmeralda, dangling a piece of paper a few inches in front of her brother's face.

"A lost pet flyer? Don't we have enough personal requests to go through? And *homework*?" reminded Atticus.

"We can always do that when we get back. That's why it's called homework," she winked. "Besides, there were lots of other missing flyers, but I only took this one. You might say it jumped out at me."

Not acknowledging her intended joke, Atticus got up from the table and walked down into the den as Esmeralda followed. This was their office. Their base of operations. Along the staircase wall were certificates of appreciation, a key to the city, a thank-you letter from the mayor, and various articles to showcase their prosperous operation of finding lost pets. And the rest of the den was stocked with all the tools for their success. A full set of animal encyclopedias, stacks of books checked out from the library, blueprints and maps of the city, and a card catalog of all their past clients. Also flashlights and hiking equipment, which sometimes were necessary in their line of work.

"Um, I don't think we're going to find it in here, Atty," said Esmeralda.

"No. But we can do a little preparation before we go," he advised.

"Not everything can be found in a book," stamped Esmeralda.

"And not everything can be found out there without it," answered Atticus.

With her arms folded, Esmeralda scuffed her shoe along the floor in an annoying fashion. It did not go unnoticed.

After flipping open some books and unrolling some papers, and feeling angry eyes on him, Atticus looked over at his sister and let out a sigh. "Don't worry, Es, I'll make it fast. Then we can get our hands dirty."

"My hands, little brother. I don't want you to fall and break that big ol' brain of yours," she smiled. And he smiled back.

Now satisfied, Esmeralda walked around the den. There was a corkboard pinned with clients whose pets they were currently working to find. Photos of various animal footprints to study. Even a funny little cat statue given to them as a gift that now acted as a paperweight, complete with a paw that moved up and down.

Stopping in front of a wall, Esmeralda looked up at a framed photo of a small white schnauzer dog. Its face was so furry that it hid its eyes and gave it a funny looking mustache. Not realizing it, she clutched the locket around her neck. The photo inside it matched the one on the wall.

Standing next to her, Atticus tried to assure her, "You know, he's probably okay. Lost dogs in this town . . . Well, any dogs in this town . . . seem to do okay. He's probably out there eating and playing and enjoying his life. Even if we haven't been able to find him yet."

"That doesn't make it any easier. No matter how many years he's been gone," she said bluntly.

Atticus placed a hand on his sister's shoulder. "And it's why we do the best we can to help others find their lost pets. So they don't have to experience what we have."

She nodded. Then spoke. "Can I help you look through some of these books?"

"I'd rather you help me check out the map," he said. "It will give us an idea where we can look."

He unrolled a giant map that covered their entire work desk and hung over to the floor. A map of Thorns Hollow. Every landmark, every area of interest. And every possible place to find a missing animal.

BILLY MOUNTAIN
- Keep on all hiking trails.
- Avoid rockslides!
- Annual mountain goat racing

WATTS MINE
- Popular for lost canaries and other treasures.
- Always bring a flashlight when riding the mine cart.

OLD HOBB GROVE
- Watch for slippery moss.
- Keep your balance and watch your step!

KURMS POND
- Local watering hole, voted #1 for frog catching.
- Bug repellent required!

CRAWLY CREEK
- Water boots needed.
- Snakes inside boots . . . most definitely not! SSSSS

7

Just a note of thanks for finding my lost dog. I hope he wasn't much treble. He always likes to play haydn go seek. Sincerely,
Jack Webster

CHAPTER 2

The sun was just starting to rise the next morning, but Atticus was already awake. As he walked down the hallway from his bedroom to the kitchen, he passed by his sister's room. Esmeralda, who seemed to take on the qualities of a bat or a sloth, was sleeping sideways across her bed. Her legs rested against the wall, pointed straight up. And the upper half of her body hung over the edge of her bed, almost upside down. Since this was nothing new, it didn't even faze her brother as he shuffled past her open door.

The Fetch family home remained quiet. Both parents were away at their jobs. Which left the twins with the responsibility to wake up, eat breakfast, and get to school on their own. It was a responsibility that seemed to come naturally to Atticus. Early to bed, early to rise. But he would have to help his sister each morning to make sure she didn't hibernate the day away. This was something he found humorous, since she always reminded him that she was born first while he "slept in." But now she made up for it by having her younger brother as her personal alarm clock.

Being up this early had its advantages though. It meant he got to see Thorns Hollow in the new light of morning each day. Putting on his sweatpants and tennis shoes, and with his house key tied around his neck, Atticus began his morning routine: a walk into town, stopping at the donut shop, and during his walk back usually finding any stray pets that got out that night.

There weren't that many people up at this early hour. Sure, there was Eddie from a few blocks over, silently riding his bike in the dark and delivering the *Hollow Herald* newspaper throughout the neighborhood. He didn't have the best throwing arm, so most papers got scattered across lawns, into trash cans, and onto roofs. But he did end up always making sure it arrived safely in the jaws of the Fetch mailbox, maybe due to the fact that Esmeralda located his missing hamster that had gotten caught in a storm drain. Atticus could also count on seeing the town sheriff in his usual favorite seat at the donut shop each morning, with a cup of joe in one hand and a half-eaten sprinkled cake donut in the other. And depending on the day, Atticus might even see Mort driving the garbage truck across town—usually with a parade of dogs following it.

After finishing his maple bar, and with the sun starting to peek over the top of the city skyline, Atticus began the walk back to his house. While the fresh air helped wake him up, and the sugar sweetness of the donuts was an added treat, it wasn't the only reason for him to follow this routine each morning. It also gave him a chance to search the city for the only missing member of the Fetch family.

Dunnsworth was given to the Fetch twins as a

fifth birthday present. At first, this white schnauzer was almost larger than the twins, and the three were nearly inseparable. Dunny followed them on fort adventures in the woods, walks through the city, and to bed at night, acting as a comfortable furry pillow as he curled up with them.

But then he was gone.

He wasn't the type to wander off. He never went outside without them. Always preferred the comforts of home, including exclusive rights to table scraps and somewhat limited fridge privileges. They didn't even have a doggie door installed at their house. Dunny would just patiently wait by the door whenever he needed to go out. And he was always fiercely protective of his family in all other regards, as his gruff voice would suggest. So it came as a shock when he went missing.

Flyers were posted.

A search throughout the city was conducted.

But days and weeks and months went by. And the family had to come to the conclusion that Dunny wouldn't be coming back. The only ones who truly couldn't accept that were the twins.

Dunnsworth was the sole reason the twins got into the pet relocation business. Not just to find him. But to help others find their own lost pets. And with a 99 percent success rate, they became the first call for many distraught families in Thorns Hollow. But they still clung to the hope they could adjust that number up to 100 percent by finding Dunny.

The twins decided to take shifts. Esmeralda, the night owl, would devote time in the evenings to search for Dunny. Atticus would take the mornings. So each time after charging up with a donut and chocolate milk, he would spend his morning walking home on a different path. A different sidewalk or different stroll through the city. Hoping to find the one spot he might've missed in order to find Dunny.

On this morning, he came up empty. But that didn't make the trip any less successful.

Atticus almost tripped over a small gray mound of fluff while exiting the donut shop. It mewed from below, rubbing against his feet, causing him to sidestep and fall to the ground. It's not often when a lost pet found him rather than the other way around. So the morning was off to a great start.

"Hi! Almost didn't notice you there. Let's see who you are," said Atticus as he found the kitten's collar. A shiny metal tag hung from it, which he read aloud.

"Puddles the Second," he announced, locating the twin Roman numerals at the end of the kitten's name tag. "You wouldn't happen to be related to Puddles the First, would you?"

The kitten stared at him innocently before sneezing repeatedly.

"If so, then I know where you belong."

The first Puddles belonged to Mister Ralph. That wasn't his last name, but it's what all the kids called him anyways. He was a retired milkman who spent his later years fishing every chance he got and sitting on the rocking chair on his front porch. With the skies clear and crisp, there was a good chance he'd be at the pier this morning.

It was slightly off his regular path, but Atticus felt it worth the trip to reunite a lost friend.

As the salt air filled his lungs, the seagulls welcomed them, circling in the air and squawking. Puddles (the Second) perched on Atticus's shoulder.

The kitten preferred not to be carried so he could enjoy the view. Waving to a few early risers hauling crab cages from the ocean, Atticus noticed a frail man seated at the far end of the pier. Wearing a long coat and floppy hat, the unshaven man turned as they approached. The creaky wooden boards of the pier announced their arrival.

"Hello, Mister Ralph. I think I have someone you lost."

"Puddles?!" exclaimed Mister Ralph. "Now where did you run off to?"

"Outside the donut shop," answered Atticus. The kitten carefully hopped off his shoulder and into the lap of his owner.

"Just because I haven't caught a bite don't mean you can just wander off to find your own," scolded Mister Ralph. "You just gotta have faith. We'll catch something yet, Puddles. And I promise you a full belly."

Atticus was ready to turn to leave, but it was obvious Mister Ralph enjoyed Atticus's company.

"How's your father been?" asked Mister Ralph.

"Pretty good. He's at work out there," answered

Atticus, wistfully looking out past the sea waves.

"I'll bet he catches more than I do," chuckled Mister Ralph as his smile revealed a few missing teeth.

"You're probably right," replied Atticus. "I'm afraid I can't really stay long though. It's a school day. And I still have to go wake up my sister."

Mister Ralph turned his attention back to his fishing pole that hung over the pier. "Say hi to Esmeralda for me. And thanks for finding this little scamp," said Mister Ralph as he petted Puddles on his head.

Atticus waved goodbye. And before he arrived back home, Puddles already had a full belly.

CHAPTER 3

Nestled along the edge of the surrounding forest was the school the Fetch twins attended, Thorns Academy, advertised as "an education amongst the pines." While Atticus enjoyed his time spent learning with his fellow students, Esmeralda always seemed more restless and distracted. Having nature just outside the windows seemed very cruel, when being stuck inside a stuffy classroom. She'd rather be outside running and climbing than chained to a desk with her nose in a book.

Esmeralda had a way of rotating through teachers like musical chairs. And all of them with funny names.

There was Missus Musslemann, a stocky lady who seemed to inhabit her name by always flexing her huge arms to make the students laugh. She'd challenge the kids to grab on to each arm as she'd lift them off the ground like weights.

Mister Subbs was a tall man with a long neck and bristly mustache. He always found himself at odds with his class, constantly having to explain he was their teacher and not a substitute. And every time he defended that accusation, his face would get flush red. Of course, it didn't help when the students would respond by yelling "Red Alert" each time, as if he were a submersible ready to dive into the ocean.

There was Mister Wright, who always found that every student in class was wrong. Seriously. The best grade anyone could get was a B. There were no As in his class. He felt that withholding perfection made everyone work harder. But most think it was just an excuse to yell at the students all the time: *"WRONNNG!"*

Missus Lipshutz liked a quiet classroom. Secretly passing notes became the only means of communication. It meant everyone was reading, studying, not talking, and definitely not asking her questions. It also meant that she could spend the day ignoring everyone if should could manage that. Of course she would normally be found seated at the back of the teachers' lounge by herself, even away from her fellow educators.

Mister Payne was the physical education teacher. And his wife, Mrs. Payne, was the school nurse. And most of the time, you'd start with one and then see the other after a sprained ankle or a bloody nose.

Mister Crump actually seemed happier than his name implied. Always polite with his students. Always joking. Always giving high fives. As long as he had his morning cup of coffee. But if he didn't . . . then look out.

For Atticus, his teacher was Miss Grobber. A portly older lady with glasses and her gray hair tied back. No student had ever correctly guessed her age, though most believed she'd been teaching longer than the academy had existed. Some even believed before the forest existed.

No one had ever seen her outside of school,

outside of the classroom, or even outside of sitting at her desk in class. As if she'd always been there and everything was just built up around her. But Atticus knew that wasn't the case.

He once rescued her scared cat from the top of a gnarly eucalyptus tree with some help. Atticus located it, while Esmeralda did the climbing and recovery. And when they brought it back to her house, she thanked them and invited both inside for some lemon squares. As they ate, she turned on her rusted metal phonograph and began to dance. It's the only time any student has ever seen her "out in the wild." And no one would believe it if he told them.

The backpack that Atticus wore to school was as big as he was. Aside from his school books, he kept a planner filled with dates and times to keep on schedule. Homework was filed according to importance and when it was due. Meetings were meticulously circled in his planner for new clients to recover their pets. And a front pouch filled with index card notes was for any last-minute student requests to locate a furry loved one.

Esmeralda of course didn't have pockets (or want them), since her brother carried everything. Without the need to be weighed down, this also made it easier for her to climb things. She could reach the top of the jungle gym in the sandbox in under five seconds. She was able to recover any lost sporting equipment from off the school roof by scaling the walls without a ladder. And she claims to have swung on the playground swing set so rapidly, that it did three complete loops, followed by a flawless dismount. Of course no one was around to see it happen, not that anyone would question her about it.

Today Atticus would have to make up a test he missed while not at school. In actuality he had been looking for flushed baby gators in the city sewer, which can be an all-day job, but thankfully he made it home before midnight. The baby reptiles' chirping gave away their location in the dark, and he was able to recover all five of them, before they could make the sewers their permanent home.

But no matter what extracurricular recovery missions he took on, it didn't get him out of his schoolwork. So he found himself in Miss Grobber's empty classroom at the end of the day to take his history exam.

But first, Atticus had to get there. And he was already running late.

As the final school bell rang and classes let out for the day, excited students spilled out into the hallways. Most of them were happy to get out of class and be done with school. Some were in a rush to catch their bus to head home, while others were looking to spend their newfound free time playing and getting into trouble.

But there were always the requests.

As Atticus navigated through the ocean of kids, he knew the very likely possibility that he would be noticed and stopped. Planning for such an occurrence, he'd need multiple options for finding his way to Miss Grobber's class without encountering any obstacles.

He mapped out alternate routes to take to avoid locker areas where the most students might be. He didn't stop at the drinking fountain to avoid making himself an easy target for small talk. Same with the restrooms, as they made openings for any kids to approach him while he washed his hands. And trying to disguise himself never worked in the past, only calling attention to the strange hat or jacket he'd wear to try to be unrecognizable. Even with all this, no matter how he tried not to be seen, he couldn't avoid it. The kids and their requests still found him.

Hey Atty, can you help me find my dog?

Atticus, have you seen my goldfish? I misplaced it at lunch.

My friend's llama ran off yesterday. Do you have the time to go look?

These were but a few of the types of requests he would get. And he'd have to politely decline. Or tell them he'd look into it later. Because if he missed taking his make-up test, he'd be in more trouble, and unable to have time for anything, including looking for lost animals.

Suddenly he found himself down the last stretch of hallway leading to class. It was empty except for a few loose school papers left behind. A crumpled piece of trash blew down the hall like a tumbleweed. A poster advertising the school lunch menu lost its adhesiveness, falling off the wall and floating down to the floor. And the faint sounds of students could be heard in the distance from outside by the school bike racks.

Atticus stood still, halfway expecting there to be some interruption. Some late straggler who would notice him from across the hallway and yell a request. Or another teacher leaving for the day might need his assistance, or worse, give him some last-minute homework assignment. But that never happened. Instead, Atticus picked up the pace, heading to Mrs. Grobber's classroom. His head swimming with memorized answers to inevitable questions for his history test. While being too distracted to remember the final obstacle in his way.

"Mister Atticus. Could I bother you for a moment?" asked a kind voice from an open doorway.

Atticus only now realized where he was. The voice came from the janitor's closet that was positioned next to Miss Grobber's classroom. And inside was Kenny, the school janitor. A gentle giant who towered over six feet tall, with thick glasses and a warm smile. The type of janitor who knew every kid in school and was instantly likable. And if you weren't careful, you'd find yourself spending all day talking to him, but enjoyably.

"Oh . . . hey, Kenny. Um, I really got to get to class for my test," replied Atticus.

"You look like you're in a hurry, but this will only take a minute," said Kenny. His hands were on his hips and he looked more concerned than normal.

Atticus nodded and stood inside the closet doorway. They both stared at the ground where he spotted one small, lonely piece of cheese. Before Kenny had a chance to explain, Atticus knew what this might be about.

"Mice?" asked Atticus, already knowing the answer.

"Yeah. There's been a few sightings," Kenny replied. "I'd like to catch them before they do too much damage. Eating school books or making too much of a mess. I just don't want to kill them if I can help it."

Atticus spoke aloud to himself, "Hmmm . . . a mouse friendly trap that won't hurt them." He looked around the room at the janitorial supplies. There were various cleaning items stacked on shelves and yard equipment leaning against the wall. Surely something in here might be able to do the job. He started to grab a few items immediately. He handed Kenny a single roll of toilet paper and an empty five-gallon bucket.

Kenny had a puzzled look on his face. "I'm not sure I quite understand, Mister Atticus."

"You can use an empty toilet paper tube. I'm sure there's probably one around here somewhere," said Atticus. "You place some of the food inside the end of it, and then place the tube at the end of a table so it hangs off it. The empty bucket goes on the floor underneath it. When the mouse enters the tube to eat, its weight will cause it to fall safely into the bucket."

"And then I can just release it outside away from the school," smiled Kenny.

Atticus reached into his backpack and removed a small container of peanut butter he had saved from lunch. "I've found this'll do the trick even better than cheese. Just a dab of it at the end of the tube, and they'll come running."

Before he left the closet, Atticus offered one more piece of advice. "You know, mice make great pets. In case you wanted to keep any."

Atticus waved as he left, took eight steps to the left, and entered the classroom next door, where a frowning Miss Grobber sat at her desk waiting for him to take his test.

CHAPTER 4

A small crowd had gathered around a large store window. As the Fetch twins approached, they could see why. Two playful puppies scurried around, chasing their tails. Each stopped long enough to stare back at the happy people who watched them. Then they continued to roll on top of each other, while biting their ears. The twins continued past the audience, who pointed and laughed at the puppies, to enter the store, walking underneath a brightly colored sign that said ZOMBIE'S PETS.

A tiny metal bell chimed as the front door

opened. When they walked inside, a cacophony of sounds greeted them. There were bellowing howls, some long meows, repeated chirps, and faint squeaks. Cages rustled and whiskers twitched in attention. An exuberant elderly man greeted them from behind the front counter.

"There's my favorite sibling sleuths!" said the man with a welcoming smile underneath his bristly mustache. He wore a knit sweater over his thin frame and had thin wisps of white hair atop his balding head.

"Hi, Mister Zoomie!" said Esmeralda. "How's business?"

"I was about to ask you both the same thing," he replied. "I can't complain. People always want a loving companion to care for."

Atticus walked over to the aquatic section. There were rows of fluorescent tanks with an assortment of fish in them. Orange clown fish hid between some of the rocks. An eel lay at the bottom of one tank, barely moving except for its lower jaw opening and closing. Small bubbles rose from a tiny pirate chest in another container as a brown-and-white-striped lionfish stared back at him, its long feathery fins swaying as it hovered. Atticus returned back to the front counter to join them.

"Any new customers we should be aware of?" asked Atticus.

"A few," said Mister Zoomie. "But don't you two worry. I provided each of them with your contact info in case any of their pets get lost."

"Thanks," said Esmeralda. She lifted a tiny bunny from its playpen to cuddle it.

"Are you two looking to add any new ones to your family?" inquired Mister Zoomie.

"Not at the moment. I think we've both got our hands full as it is," said Atticus. He looked over to find his sister had fallen into the playpen and was underneath a pile of playful cottontails.

"Well, just let me know. And I'll be happy to waive the adoption fee," said Mister Zoomie.

Atticus was prepared to provide his sister a hand to help her out of the playpen, but she hopped out instead. And with a kindly wave, they departed the store to continue their errands.

Next they stopped at some apartments located above Mario's Deli. They didn't even have to look at the registry, since they were familiar with one specific resident. After pressing a buzzer to be let in, they climbed up the stairs to apartment 555.

"Every time I see this number, it looks like *SSSSS*," joked Esmeralda, pursing her lips together as she sprayed to make its sound.

"That makes sense," agreed Atticus. "Especially considering who lives here."

They knocked at the door and waited. After about a minute, the door slowly opened the few inches that the lock chain would allow, and an eyeball looked out. Once they were recognized, the door closed shut, and reopened all the way.

"Hey dude and dudette!" said Tod. "I wasn't expecting company. Come on in but watch your step!"

They entered the small cramped studio apartment. The worn-down couch doubled as a bed. There were clothing and discarded food containers all over the floor. The kitchen was hidden away in a tiny alcove, with dirty dishes stacked up in the sink. And Tod slumped back onto the couch very comfortably. He wore his hair long enough to cover his eyes, while a small goatee of hair clung to his chin. His shirt was baggy, and his pants were long and frayed, resting over his bare feet.

"To what do I owe your wonderful visit?" he cordially asked while also sounding confused.

"Just a follow-up consultation," said Atticus. "We wanted to see how Jake was doing."

"Right over there," said Tod, pointing behind him.

In the corner of the room, between the broken heater and the cracked widow, was a giant glass tank. And inside of it, wrapped up in a serpentine pile, was an enormous boa constrictor. There were also a few stacks of heavy encyclopedias resting on top of the tank.

"He can't get out again after I put those books on top," said Tod. "I figured I wasn't readin' them, so they work great."

"Snakes are incredibly strong and have a habit of getting out of tight places. Make sure to keep heavy things on there so he doesn't push open the lid. We don't want him to escape like last time," warned Atticus.

"Remind me again where you found him?" asked Tod in a haze.

Esmeralda happily chimed in, "The pizza oven!"

"Actually it was on top of it. After sliding down five flights of stairs, Jake found the closest warm spot in the restaurant kitchen. Mario wasn't too happy to see Jake, so he gave us the call."

"Ohhhhh, right! I guess that's why I'm banned from eating there," said Tod.

"You and Jake both," smiled Esmeralda.

Atticus looked at his wristwatch with a nervous glance. There was one last stop they had to make, and he was in a rush to get there.

"This concludes our consultation," said Atticus as he nudged his sister toward the door.

"See ya later, Tod!" shouted Esmeralda as they ran down the hall to the stairs.

"Not if we see you first!" replied Tod. He looked around the room at the empty food containers in stunned silence. "Now what am I gonna eat today? Oh, I know . . . there's always Italian food!"

The Fetch twins walked at a hurried pace over the sidewalks and side streets of downtown on the way to a meeting. With each person they came in contact with, their reputation proceeded them. They passed by multiple businesses who waved at them, as cars honked along the street, bringing a smile to their faces.

They noticed along the base of each building were bowls filled with water and some with treats, as a courtesy to their furry-footed community. They didn't have time to stop for anyone as they raced to their appointment.

"Did you bring enough with you?" asked Esmeralda, with her brother following behind.

"Yes," answered Atticus, thumbing his stack of business cards in his front pocket. "Although we probably only need just one for this meeting."

They stopped in front of the entrance to the glass building. It was made entirely out of reflective windows. There were no bowls of water or treats placed outside. But there weren't any flowers or landscaping either. This building was all business, which gave off a coldness to it. But it was also why they were here. To expand their customer base.

The doorman positioned outside instantly recognized them. He held open the door for them to enter. Before they could thank him, he was the one doing the thanking. "You probably don't remember, but about a month ago, you helped my daughter with her—"

"Pet mouse, Sergeant Sniffs!" interrupted Atticus. "Of course we do. Mice have a habit of chewing out of their cages."

Esmeralda continued, "A few food crumbs were all that was needed to get him back."

The doorman nodded, then pointed to the elevator inside the hallway. "You'll be going up to the fifth floor. They'll check you in at the desk when you arrive," he said. "And thanks again for finding Sarge!"

"Can't we take the stairs?" asked Atticus.

"The elevator will be faster," she replied.

The elevator was empty as they entered it. Which was probably a good thing, because as soon as the doors closed, Atticus's breathing became labored.

"Just five floors, Atty," assured Esmeralda. "I'll count them with you. One . . . two . . ."

"That's okay," gasped Atticus, trying to breathe slowly. "Saying it out loud doesn't really help."

Atticus didn't like the enclosed space of an elevator. Even when it's filled with people.

And much more so when it has to move. His breathing gets heavy. He sweats and feels nauseous. Until the doors would reopen and his bout of claustrophobia would pass. Esmeralda joked it's because they shared the same enclosed space before they were born. She might be right.

As the elevator dinged and the doors slowly slid open, Atticus was the first one off, stepping into the hallway of the fifth floor. As he bent over to regain his breath, Esmeralda walked past him toward the front desk. The secretary stopped her work and immediately greeted them.

"You're here for your appointment with Mister Statly," said the secretary. "In through the door on your right."

When they entered the office, they found a middle-aged man hunched over his desk. There were stacks of folders on one side, and he was thumbing through paperwork in front of him. He scribbled something down on a notepad, and without looking up, spoke to the room.

"Have a seat in front of me. I'll just be a minute."

Atticus and Esmeralda sat down on two chairs facing his desk. Their feet barely touching the floor.

Esmeralda elbowed a reminder to Atticus, who pulled out one of the business cards and held it in his hand, waiting for the right moment.

As the man put down his pencil, he finally looked up at his two guests with a blank expression.

"Before you try to go through your rehearsed pitch, I've got a question for you. What is your yield?" asked Mister Statly.

Swallowing before he spoke, Atticus replied, "I'm not sure I understand."

"Your yield? What is your return on investment?" continued Mister Statly, starting to get more impatient. "How good is your record?"

"Our pet relocation services have a ninety-nine percent success rate," said Esmeralda proudly. But her pride got quickly squashed.

"I see . . . " spoke Mister Statly, starting to trail off as he penciled in that number onto his notepad. "But not perfect. And why is that?"

Atticus noticed his sister grasp her locket from around her neck. He quickly answered, "I'm not sure any job can have a one hundred percent success rate."

"Mine can," snapped Mister Statly. "I do that all the time. Sometimes even higher than that."

"That's impossible," frowned Esmeralda.

"Look kids . . . as an accountant I deal in numbers. Making everything balance. To achieve this perfection, I also look for it in others. But go ahead, give me your pitch."

Atticus took a breath and then spoke. "Our pet relocation services have a high success rate. Almost perfect."

"*Almost,*" whispered Mister Statly under his breath.

"We're branching out to offer our services to new clients who we haven't spoken with in the past," said Atticus, handing him their business card. When Mister Statly didn't take it from him after a long, uncomfortable pause, Atticus just placed it at the top of his desk.

"I will not be requiring your services at this time. Or probably ever," said Mister Statly. "I don't even own a pet. I find them to be a nuisance. Too much responsibility."

"Then why do you live in this city?!" shouted Esmeralda, who stormed out of the office.

Atticus sheepishly stood up to leave, but then turned back around.

"In case you change your mind, you have our card," said Atticus as he exited the office to follow his sister.

Atticus rejoined his sister, who paced in front of the elevator. A soft voice spoke behind them.

"Hey kids—I have a pet. An African gray parrot," said the secretary. "I named him Chortle, for the funny laugh he makes."

"Those birds are great at mimicking humans," said Atticus.

"And my other pets too," she added. "He's silent whenever we're in the room with him. He'll saddle up against the edge of the cage and just listen."

"But when you leave the room?" asked Atticus.

"He barks. And meows," she laughed. "I never thought I'd own a bird that was also part dog and part cat."

The elevator door dinged open, and Esmeralda stepped inside and held it for her brother.

"Can I have one of your cards?" asked the secretary.

"Absolutely," offered Atticus. "And I hope you never have to use it."

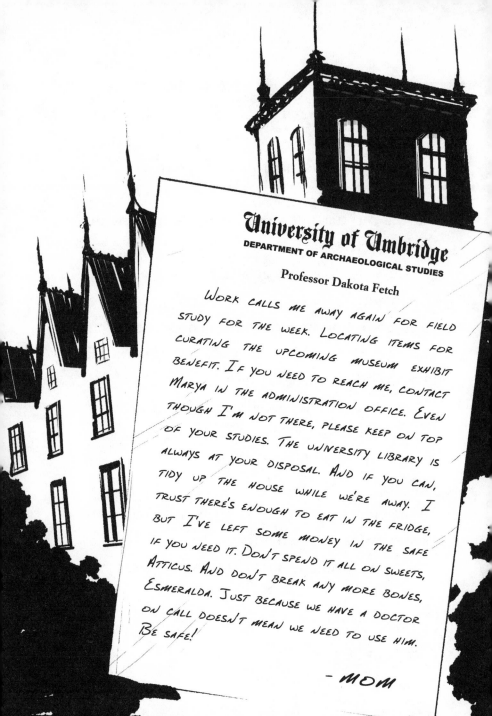

University of Umbridge
DEPARTMENT OF ARCHAEOLOGICAL STUDIES

Professor Dakota Fetch

WORK CALLS ME AWAY AGAIN FOR FIELD STUDY FOR THE WEEK. LOCATING ITEMS FOR CURATING THE UPCOMING MUSEUM EXHIBIT BENEFIT. IF YOU NEED TO REACH ME, CONTACT MARYA IN THE ADMINISTRATION OFFICE. EVEN THOUGH I'M NOT THERE, PLEASE KEEP ON TOP OF YOUR STUDIES. THE UNIVERSITY LIBRARY IS ALWAYS AT YOUR DISPOSAL. AND IF YOU CAN, TIDY UP THE HOUSE WHILE WE'RE AWAY. I TRUST THERE'S ENOUGH TO EAT IN THE FRIDGE, BUT I'VE LEFT SOME MONEY IN THE SAFE IF YOU NEED IT. DON'T SPEND IT ALL ON SWEETS, ATTICUS. AND DON'T BREAK ANY MORE BONES, ESMERALDA. JUST BECAUSE WE HAVE A DOCTOR ON CALL DOESN'T MEAN WE NEED TO USE HIM. BE SAFE!

- MOM

This is to certify that:
DAKOTA FETCH and KOPI

Have successfully completed the pilot and copilot training program and flight requirements for private pilots as prescribed by the Aviation Administration; and has the aeronautical knowledge that meets or surpasses the minimum requirements set forth for small planes.

Certified by:

International Morse Code Translator

A	·—	N	—·	1	·————	
B	—···	O	———	2	··———	
C	—·—·	P	·——·	3	···——	
D	—··	Q	——·—	4	····—	
E	·	R	·—·	5	·····	
F	··—·	S	···	6	—····	
G	——·	T	—	7	——···	
H	····	U	··—	8	———··	
I	··	V	···—	9	————·	
J	·———	W	·——	0	—————	
K	—·—	X	—··—	.	·—·—·—	
L	·—··	Y	—·——	,	——··——	
M	——	Z	——··	?	··——··	

\-\- \-\-\- \-\- / \-. \-\-\- \- / \-.... .\- \-.\-. \-.\- / \-.\-\-. .\- \-

mom not back yet

.. / \-\- .. \-\-. .... \- / \-.... . .\- \- / ... . .\-. / .... \-\-\- \-\- .

I might beat her home

.\-\-\- .. \-.. \- / \- \-\-\- / \-.... .. \-\-. / ..\- .\-\-. /
\-\- \-\-\- .\-. . / ....\-. .\-. \-\-\- \-\- / \-\-\- \-.\-. . .\-. \-.

Want to dig up more from ocean

.. ....\-. / .\-\-\- . / \-.\-. .\- \-. / .\- \-... \-\-\- .. \-... /
... \- \-\-\- .\-. \-\-

if we can avoid storm

\-.\-. .\-.. . .\- \-. / ..\- .\-\-. / \-.... .\- ... . \-\- . \-.. \- /
\-.... . ....\-. \-\-\- .\-. . / .. / \-\-. . \- / \-.... .\- \-.\-. \-.\-/

clean up basement before I get back

... . / \-.\-\-. \-\-\- ..\- / \-.\-. .. \-.. ... / ... \-\-\- \-\-\- \-. /

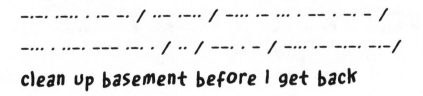

Long thought lost at sea, the sunken ship of Thorns Hollow's own "Cross-eye" Cristov the Corsair has been located off the East Coast. Using outdated maps and the recovered journal written in the infamous pirate's own blood, Garrison Fetch was able to find the ship in a deep trench twenty-three miles from shore. He will now take the next week to raise the ship from the depths and salvage whatever remains of the abandoned pirate gold entombed in the belly of the ship. Fetch continues to add to his impressive record for the most salvage recoveries on the open seas in this region.

Professor Dakota Fetch had help in finding her latest archaeological discovery during her sabbatical trip to the Amazon rain forest. While digging for bones, her four-footed copilot, Kopi, was able to root out the hidden statue of the lost tribe. "He keeps me company," joked Fetch. "But every now and then, he's a better navigator on land then he is in the air." Finding this statue could mean more items will be added to the *Lost Civilization* exhibit that the museum is curating. But the professor only has a few days left to search, as classes begin at the university on Monday.

Mayor awards business achievement award to Atticus and Esmeralda Fetch after recovering lost mayoral pet. The twins continue to follow in the family business of finding lost things.

CHAPTER 5

"**Esmeralda!** I've heard back from Mom and Dad. Es, where are you?"

Atticus wandered the house looking for his sister, realizing she was nowhere to be found. Of course, she might be in the perfect hiding place, just waiting to jump out and muss up his hair. But he checked all her usual spots, including under his bed, and found nothing. He checked the trees in the backyard, the trees in the neighbor's yard, and all the other trees in the neighborhood. She wasn't climbing on any of them either. He was going to need some help.

He went to his neighbor across the street, Mister Chauncy. He was a long-retired detective who lived alone except for one roommate. Atticus rang the doorbell and heard a patter of feet approach.

"Hello Atticus. Do you require my services?" asked the elder detective.

"Actually I was hoping for his," answered Atticus, pointing near the man's feet. "Can I borrow your dog?"

"What do you think, Boonie?" asked Mister Chauncy. "You've got yourself a job!"

Boone Dog was a droopy-eyed bloodhound. The sweetest companion one could have. And he had a great nose. If anyone could help find Atticus's sister, it would be this hound.

Together they returned to the Fetch house. With his nose to the floor, Boone Dog bounded ahead to take in his surroundings. Atticus helped steer him toward his sister's bedroom.

"Have a good sniff, Boone," said Atticus, watching the dog rummage through her piles of clothes. He then ran down the hall as Atticus followed.

"Do you have her scent, boy?" asked Atticus.

Boone Dog stopped into the kitchen. He was just tall enough to push his nose against the lower cupboard and press his paw against it to open. His search had ended. He didn't find Esmeralda. But he did find an open box of dog treats, and proceeded to knock it over, spilling out its contents.

As Boone chewed each biscuit down to the last crumb, Atticus shook his head. "I guess this means you're retired too."

He returned the dog back to his owner across the street. Mister Chauncy stood in the doorway to greet them. "Find what you were looking for?"

"He did. But I didn't," replied Atticus. Boone Dog's droopy eyes looked up at his owner and the dog licked his lips. "Thanks anyways."

As Atticus turned to leave, the detective stopped him. "Sometimes when you least expect it, what you're looking for can find you first." Mister Chauncy pointed to a sticky note stuck on the back of his neighbor's shirt.

Atticus removed the note and thanked his neighbor before returning home. The sticky note was addressed to him.

How did she stick it on my back without me noticing? he wondered. One of life's mysteries. But at least now he had a clue where to go look.

"The Dig" was exactly what it sounded like. A giant dirt pit on the edge of town. At one time it was where old cars went to die. A junkyard. But it also was used in the past as a trash pile, a tire yard, and even an excavation area for the college Archaeological Department. Many a trip was taken to join his mother and her class of students.

Not much was ever dug up from there. Maybe a random petrified shark's tooth left over from where the ocean once was. Sometimes the last remnants of some rubber tires that burnt off and were discarded.

Old unrecycled car parts. Or random bags of trash you wouldn't dare look through.

After taking two bus connections to get out to The Dig, he wandered up to the edge of the pit. And sure enough, down below at the base of it stood Esmeralda. She held a shovel in one hand and some weathered old paper in the other.

"Ahoy down there!" Atticus shouted, peeking over the edge.

"Thar be that a scallywag or me brother? I know not the difference," she replied. "Come on down and join me, Atty!"

Atticus pondered her offer. The Dig had a slight incline to it. It wasn't a walk through the park to get to the bottom. More like a run through the dirt. And he didn't like his chances that he'd make it unscathed.

"I'm fine up here!" shouted Atticus.

Esmeralda frowned. "You'll never get anywhere up there, little brother. Come on!"

Atticus gingerly took a step down. Then another. And another. Soon he was picking up speed and couldn't stop. He began to run down the steep slope, wailing as he ran, until he reached the bottom. But he couldn't stop himself, and rolled across the dirt like a tumbleweed, stopping at the feet of his sister.

"I guess that's one way to do it," she said, offering him a hand to help him up.

As Atticus got back to his feet, he brushed off his clothes, making a cloud of dirt around him. He shook his head. "Next time, stay home. It would make things so much easier for me. And far less dirty."

"Sometimes it's more fun to get your nose out of a book and get your hands dirty," she told him.

"It's not my hands I'm worried about," he replied. "It's the rest of me that's covered in it."

"That's the spirit!" exclaimed Esmeralda. "Now follow along and help me look."

They walked over to a section of dirt that was undisturbed. It was at this point that Atticus looked around The Dig. There were dozens of empty holes dug up all around them. And whatever she was looking for, she'd been unsuccessful.

"Use that big ol' brain of yours and help me decipher this," she ordered, handing Atticus the mangled paper in her hands.

"What's this supposed to be?" he asked.

"I don't know. Some kind of treasure map I think," she replied. "But it doesn't really give any coordinates."

Atticus turned the map sideways, trying to make heads or tails of it. "So you've just been out here digging randomly?"

"I figure eventually I'll find it . . . whatever it is," she answered.

"Where did you find this map? You didn't steal it, did you?" he asked.

Esmeralda shook her head proudly. "Nope. I made it."

Now Atticus was perplexed. "Wait . . . what?!"

"Yeah, I can't even read my own writing. Or my own drawings," she laughed.

Atticus slapped the top of his forehead. *So there's nothing out here after all.*

Esmeralda stuck her boot on the edge of her shovel and began to dig a new hole. As Atticus tried to stop her from wasting more time, she just chucked the dirt at him. Every time he asked her to stop was met with more dirt thrown his way, until he got the message. He stepped out of the way and remained quiet.

CLANK

Esmeralda's eyes widened at the metallic sound her shovel made. It had struck something hidden in the dirt.

"Don't just stand there. Help out," she instructed.

Atticus crouched down and began to dig and push away the loose dirt with his hands. He sifted around the edges of the object until it began to reveal its shape. It was a metal cylinder of some kind. A few feet wide. And it took both of them to lift it from the hole.

"*X* marks the spot!" she shouted, cackling like a pirate.

"More like *ES*," he replied with a grin.

"What do you think it is?" she asked.

"Let's find out!" said Atticus.

He found a hatch and tried to open it, but the metal had rusted shut. Esmeralda was already trying to lift the heavy cylinder over her head when Atticus pointed at the shovel instead. She chipped away at the hatch until it broke off. Then she carefully opened the metal container.

Inside was an old yellowed newspaper article, too faded to read except for a few words that could be pieced together: *pioneer* and *convoy*. There also appeared to be some old horse spurs and tools of some kind. Some flint used for a hunting rifle. And something that looked like an empty metal can of food rations.

"Well that was a bust. Let's go," said Esmeralda, already picking up her shovel to leave.

"Wait! Don't you know what these are?" he asked her.

"Wastes of time," she replied.

"No!" he said, almost offended. "These appear to be artifacts from our ancestors. It's like a time capsule from the early days of Thorns Hollow. I'm not sure how old, but maybe late 1800s. You made quite a find! Why aren't you more interested?"

Esmeralda turned back to her brother and placed her hands on his shoulders, ready to impart her sage wisdom to her younger sibling. "Life is the adventure, Atty. Not the treasure."

Even going against how he really felt, he allowed her to be right this time. As Esmeralda started to climb out of The Dig, her brother closed the capsule and returned it to the ground, filling the hole back up with dirt. It now was for someone else to find.

Riding the bus back home, Esmeralda turned to her brother. "Atty, besides the note I left for you, why did you come out here to look for me?"

"We have chores to do," he answered.

"Chores?" she groaned. "Next time, leave me with the buried treasure."

The door to the basement slowly creaked open, as light from the hallway cast long shadows down the stairway to the bottom.

"We don't really have to clean the basement," said Esmeralda, standing behind her brother.

Atticus disagreed. "It's what Dad told us."

"Well I don't think he really meant it. It's just something you say to someone to keep them busy and out of trouble," said Esmeralda.

Atticus smiled. "It's good advice, then. Come on."

Atticus took a few steps down the old wooden staircase. He instinctively reached his hand up to grab the cord to the lightbulb, but it was just out of reach. Esmeralda stretched over him and easily snapped the cord to turn it on.

"Now I see why you need me," she smirked, walking past him to the bottom of the stairs.

"Maybe one day, I'll be as tall as you," whined Atticus. "Maybe even taller."

"Keep growing little brother and we'll see."

The basement was littered with boxes of every size, enormous constructed crates, and furniture with dusty sheets hanging over them. It appeared to be storage for everything that wouldn't fit in the house that had nowhere else to go.

"Atty, look over there," cried Esmeralda. "It's a missing eight legged pet!!" A small spider slowly crawled between a crack in the wall and disappeared.

Atticus shook his head as his sister laughed.

"What are we even supposed to do with all of this?" asked Esmeralda.

Atticus turned to leave. "I'll go find some brooms. Just don't make a mess until I get back."

Esmeralda shouted at her brother as he climbed the stairs, "Too late—it's already messy!"

She began to walk around the basement, in between all the obstacles in her way. She made a game of it. With so many closed boxes and everything hidden under sheets, it was like one big surprise party with gifts waiting to be opened.

Pulling on the lid of a crate until the nails pried loose, she tumbled inside of it, head over heels. She landed into some packaging hay which made for a crunchy bristly fall. As she balanced to stand back up, she was able to swivel the item contained in the crate. It was made out of thick metal and too heavy to lift. But a removable piece was next to it that fit inside the barrel. A blunted metal harpoon. Something that might attach to a ship.

"That belongs to Dad," she surmised.

Another rectangular box behind it seemed like it might be tougher to open. It had a rusty padlock attached to it, with no key in sight. But her boot might do the trick. Esmeralda kicked at it repeatedly as the lock shifted back and forth. One last well- placed kick knocked it off the stack and onto the floor, jarring the lock loose. The lid fell open and something tumbled out of it. She lifted up the oval item to have a look at it when her brother returned.

"Handle with care," warned Atticus, pointing at the written words on the open box.

"Where were you when I was trying to open this?" joked Esmeralda, who held up the item to cover her face. "How do I look?"

"Silly. Put it back carefully and take this," ordered Atticus, handing her a broom.

She placed the tribal mask back into the box before grabbing the broom from her brother.

"That's one of Mom's," announced Esmeralda.

"That's why you should be more careful. It might belong to the museum," reasoned Atticus.

They began to sweep the dust around the room. Atticus on one side and Esmeralda beginning to wander off to the other side. She approached a giant bookcase filled with dusty tomes. None of which she cared to read. But the item she was more interested in was the skull just out of reach on the very top shelf.

With her brother not paying attention, she had her opportunity. This would be easier than scaling the trees in the backyard, as the shelves offered perfect climbing to get to the top. With one boot over the other, she began her ascent. Four shelves up and a half dozen left to go.

She was right. The climb was easy. She grabbed the skull, but as she started to pull, it released a cloud of dust which she inhaled. As she sneezed, her fingers lost their grip, and she fell backward. But a plastic covered sofa chair cushioned her fall. It also let out a squeaking sound that alerted her brother. Some of the loosened books from the shelf rained down to the floor, with one falling directly into her lap.

"What did I tell you about being careful?" scolded Atticus. "You're making more of a mess than what we started with, if that's even possible. What were you trying to do?"

Esmeralda didn't have an answer. She had already forgotten about the skull. She was now more interested in the book that had fallen into her lap. Or rather, what was inside of it. Hidden between the pages was a piece of worn paper that peeked out from the middle of the book. Something stashed in there and forgotten . . . until now.

CHAPTER 6

On the edge of the city stood a very old, tall Victorian house. It had at least three stories to it. There were pointed spires like spears attached to the roof in multiple areas. And it stood out like a sore thumb, once you knew where to look.

"Have you ever been this way before?" asked Esmeralda.

"Never. I didn't even know it existed," replied Atticus. "Even walking here, it seemed like a dead-end road."

"So that's it, then," said Esmeralda. "It's kinda creepy . . . I like it."

"Let's go find out to be sure," said her brother.

There was a rough path that lead up to the front door. The lawn around it grew wild and unattended. And the house itself looked dark. Abandoned. No driveway and no vehicles. No people around at all. Not even a mailbox. There were no signs of life.

The steps leading up to the house creaked under their feet, as if being touched for the first time. The wood splintered as they put weight on it.

There was no welcome mat outside. No doorbell to be found. The blinds were drawn on every window so no one could see in or out. There wasn't any hint of light inside.

Atticus made a fist and lightly knocked on the door. He listened and waited.

Nothing.

"That's no way to get their attention," she told her brother as she pounded on the door even harder and kicked it with her boot. If anyone were inside, they definitely heard that.

The sound of the doorknob was being fumbled from inside. Then the knob turned and the door began to open.

A man answered by cracking the door slightly ajar and peering out. The thick glasses on his face hid his eyes. His shoulder length hair was fair in color, with a full beard that was starting to turn white. When he swung open the door, he revealed a scholarly tweed suit. He also looked annoyed.

"We—we—don't want any," he stammered.

"Want any what?" asked Atticus.

"Well . . . whatever it is you're trying to sell. Or trying to sign me up for," explained the man, who seemed distracted as he kept looking over his shoulder.

Appearing beside him was a familiar large brown boxer dog.

"Maxwell?" asked Esmeralda.

Upon hearing his name, the dog wagged its tail.

"How do you know him?" asked the man with a stern voice. "And who are you?"

"I'm Atticus and this is my sister, Esmeralda."

The annoyed man continued his line of questioning. "And who are your parents?"

"We're the Fetch family. Maybe you've heard of us," said Esmeralda.

The man let out a grunt.

Esmeralda handed him the missing dog flyer. He adjusted his glasses as he looked at it and let out another grunt. He looked down at Maxwell, who stared up at him.

"You don't look missing to me, boy. Sorry you came all this way for nothing."

As he prepared to close the door on them, Esmeralda stopped him. "So he was never lost? Then why is there this flier?"

Over the man's shoulder, an older lady entered the room. She also had light hair, almost white, and shoulder length. She also wore glasses. She was carrying a suitcase and supplies, wearing clothing that made it appear they were going on safari.

She gave the man an impatient look. The man hurried to finish the conversation.

"I'm Professor Hadrick Mordred and that is Doctor Persephone Mordred, my wife. And you're keeping us from our field trip. Now if you don't mind—"

"Where are you going?" asked Esmeralda with a devilish smile, knowing the delay would further irritate him.

"None of your concern!" And with that, he slammed the door shut in their face.

As the twins began to walk home, Esmeralda couldn't help but notice: "We found that missing pet in record time."

Maybe so. But Atticus wondered why this didn't feel resolved.

As they walked home, Atticus had an idea. "Change of plans, sis. We're headed downtown. Do you have your bus pass on you?"

"You never let me leave home without reminding me," she answered. "But why does this suddenly feel like homework?"

Not waiting long at the bus stop, they caught the next one and found seats in the back.

"When are you going to tell me where we're going?" Esmeralda asked.

"The county records office," Atticus answered. "They keep the most complete residential records for everyone in town. It's the only way for us to be sure who the Mordreds are. And if we hurry, we can make it to the office before they close."

After exiting the bus, they ran toward the

downtown building and up two flights of stairs and arrived before the county worker could lock the door. The twins walked up to the counter where the slightly perturbed employee addressed them.

"You got in just under the wire but you'll have to make this quick," the employee said, pulling on his thin mustache. "What are you looking for?"

"Residential records that cover the last one hundred years," Atticus blurted out.

"Very well. Follow me," said the employee.

They walked down a passage of vaulted ceilings with high shelves and thick books. The employee seemed to know this specific location like the back of his hand, stopping exactly in front of a shelf where he proceeded to pull the book from. The tome was as tall as it was wide, and almost as big as the twins themselves.

"I assume you want me to carry it for you as well," asked the employee rhetorically.

"If you may do us the utmost pleasure," Esmeralda sarcastically responded with a curtsy.

"*Hmpf!*" grunted the employee.

He brought the book to a wooden podium and

placed it atop. He turned on the attached desk lamp and turned back toward the twins.

"I'm afraid you'll have to turn the pages yourselves," he said snidely. "When you are done, simply leave it here and then exit. I'll give you fifteen minutes."

Before he could ask, Esmeralda crouched down so Atticus could sit on her shoulders. When she stood back up, Atticus could reach the podium to open the book. After a quick scan of the directory, he feverishly turned alphabetical pages until he reached the section for *M*-named residents.

"Find anything?" asked Esmeralda.

"There's a lot of names here. One hundred years' worth!" he exclaimed.

He continued to look. They could hear the employee loudly cough near the front desk to remind them they were running out of time.

"Anything now?!" she asked again impatiently.

"You can let me down," he told her.

They walked past the front desk. Esmeralda gave him the thumbs-up. The employee squinted as he followed them out, then he locked the door behind them.

Esmeralda prodded her brother. "So?"

"Anyone that's ever lived in Thorns Hollow this century was in that book. But the Mordreds weren't even listed," he said in a defeated tone. "It doesn't make any sense. It's like they don't exist."

"Next time, check the records for the 1800s. Maybe they're vampires," Esmeralda joked. Atticus remained deep in thought. "Or maybe they're running from the government to avoid paying taxes. That would be secretive! There's also witness protection. They've been given new identities after stumbling across some secret too dangerous to reveal. Heck, they might even be kooky time travelers. Right?"

"Never mind," groaned Atticus. He wasn't taking this defeat lightly. He was quiet the whole bus ride home.

"You know who might know them? Mom and Dad," offered Esmeralda.

"You're . . . *right!*" exclaimed Atticus. He immediately sat up straight with a renewed sense of purpose.

Inside the Fetch family home office, he began drafting a letter to their mom. While out in the field, she always wanted an update from them. And he could use that as a means to ask her. He sealed the letter and stuck a note on it for his mother's class assistant. He placed it inside a small cylindrical container, then placed that into the pneumatic tube against the wall. Each tube went out to a different location in order to contact their parents. With a sudden burst of air pressure, this one would directly shoot the letter toward the university's Archaeological Office, where they'd have additional means for it to reach their mom.

As much traveling as she did for the university and museum, it meant that she'd have to log in those locations in advance. Marya had a system in place to get any messages to her by the fastest means possible. "Air mail." But not by plane.

Atop the university clock tower was the school's aviary, run by the Ornithology Department. Any outgoing messages could be sent from here, using a wide array of birds. Enclosed in cages were an assortment that included the usual homing pigeons and doves, but also Canadian geese, a hawk, some black ravens, a feisty hummingbird, seagulls, a hungry pelican, a stork, and the arctic tern (which was considered to have the longest migration distance for its trip from the Arctic to the Antarctic).

Their mom would receive their message shortly, while their father would get his sent by telegraph. And, hopefully, they could help clear up the mystery of the Mordreds.

Marya—
Please forward
this letter to
our mom to
read. Thanks

Mom,

Before you ask, I recently got a perfect score with extra credit on my history exam. Even Esmeralda has been finishing her reading assignments before climbing the trees in the backyard. So everything

has been going well with our studies. And no broken bones either!

But something else concerns us. While cleaning out the basement, we found an old flyer. Do you know anything about a missing dog that belonged to the Mordreds? It's not a family we're familiar with. And

they weren't exactly helpful when we went over to talk to them. In fact, they were pretty hurried and rude. Do you or Dad know them at all?

Sincerely,
Atticus (and Esmeralda)

.... --- .--. . / -.-- --- ..- / .- .-. . / -.. --- .. -. --.

/ .-- . .-.. .-.. / -.. .- -..

hope you are doing well dad

-- . / .... .- ...- . / .- / --.- ..- . ... - .. --- -.

we have a question

.-- .... --- / .- .-. . / - .... . / -- --- .-. -.. .-. . -.. ...

who are the mordreds

-- --- -- / .. ... / .- ...- --- .. -.. .. -. --. /

--.- ..- . ... - .. --- -.

mom is avoiding question

.-- . / - .... .. -. -.- / -.-- --- ..- / -... --- - .... /

-.- -. --- .-- / - .... . --

we think you both know them

.-- .... -.-- / -.-- . . .--. / ... . -.-. .-. . -

CHAPTER 7

Atticus laid back on his bed, staring at the ceiling, deep in thought. Whenever he needed a moment to clear his mind, this was his spot. The still surroundings and quiet room could sometimes help him arrive at some type of clarity. But in this case, he had been staring for hours with no results. And he didn't even notice how long his sister had been standing in the doorway.

"What's on your mind?" asked Esmeralda, holding her hands behind her back.

"Nothing, and that's what worries me," answered Atticus. "I mean, I can't shake the thought that something was off about the Mordreds."

"At least they have a cool dog," said Esmeralda.

"So how come we've never seen or heard of him before? Or their family for that matter? We kind of know everyone. Or everyone knows us," reminds Atticus.

"Even Mom and Dad haven't said a peep, which is unlike them."

"About that," replied Esmeralda. "This just arrived in the mail."

She revealed a letter she was holding behind her back. It was the letter they originally sent out to their mom. The envelope arrived back unopened with a RETURN TO SENDER mark stamped on it.

"You know Mom. She might be somewhere off the map, unable to be reached," shrugged Esmeralda.

Or she might be avoiding the question, thought Atticus. "You know Mom . . ."

Esmeralda grabbed her brother by the wrist. "Let's go check out the telegraph machine. Who knows. Maybe Dad left us a message."

Atticus perked up at the thought and followed his sister into the den where the machine sat. A paper message did arrive, and they unspooled it from the machine. Atticus sat hunched over the desk and translated it before leaning back in his chair.

"What does it say?" asked Esmeralda.

Holding the paper, he read his father's short answers:

where did you find that flyer

I do not know anything about that dog

leave the mordreds alone

Now Esmeralda was confused and getting mad. "That's it?!"

Atticus remained silent. Defeated.

"You're right, little brother. Something strange is going on. I guess it's up to us to solve it."

A faint scratching sound was coming from the front door. They looked at each other, both coming to the same conclusion. They raced to open the front door. Awaiting them outside was Maxwell, panting, and wagging his tail.

They invited the dog into the house as he nuzzled up against Esmeralda.

"It's good to see you too," she responded happily as Maxwell knocked her over onto her back to give her wet kisses.

In their line of work, being around so many animals, one is prepared for anything. So Atticus went over to the kitchen counter and washed out two bowls in the sink. With one, he filled it with water. With the other, he opened a can of dog food from the cabinet and poured it in. Before he could place both bowls on the ground, Maxwell inhaled the food and lapped up the water, splashing it all over their shoes. It had been awhile since they had a dog in their kitchen. And they couldn't help but think of Dunnsworth.

"You know what this means," winked Esmeralda. "Now we're going to have to return him back to the Mordreds."

Atticus rubbed his chin as something more concerning popped into his mind.

"But more importantly, who leaves their dog alone when going away on a trip?"

Atticus opened a bottom drawer in the kitchen. It was deep enough to hold a lot of random useful items, but also very unorganized. There were packages of half-opened batteries for flashlights, masking tape, rubber bands, rulers, a hammer, marking pens, loose paperclips, a pair of sunglasses, and more oddities. But as he dug through it, shifting the items around, he was having a hard time finding what he wanted.

"I can't find any spare dog leashes," he told his sister.

"Maxwell doesn't need one," she answered. "He got here safely on his own. All we have to do is walk him home. I'm sure it'll be okay."

"You're probably right," he surmised.

"Probably?" She felt slightly insulted. "Of course I'm right. I'm your big sister."

Thorns Hollow had very loose leash laws compared to most cities. Given the preponderance of pets that lived here, it was a very relaxed rule. And maybe the reason why so many pets went missing. Still, whenever given the choice, Atticus always liked to err on the side of caution. But it was a short enough walk they'd have to make, so it shouldn't be a problem.

Atticus smiled as he pushed the drawer closed. Maxwell watched them while waiting patiently by the front door. His cheek flaps starting to salivate. After stuffing his pockets full of chewable biscuits for their walk, Atticus tossed one to Maxwell, who snapped it out of the air and instantly swallowed it. The trio began their return trip to the Mordreds.

The walk begun quite uneventfully. They passed through quiet neighborhoods with very little traffic. One resident was watering his lawn and offered up his hose so Maxwell could drink. Another elderly couple sat on their front porch in rocking chairs, watching them walk by.

They made it to Spitty Bridge in record time. This old wooden bridge was slightly out of the way, but offered a more comfortable walk across to the area where the Mordreds lived. It also was a hangout for kids looking to waste time by competing to see who could hold their drool over the edge before it dripped into the lake. Two kids had just finished a competition as they passed by.

"Hey, is that your dog?" one of them asked Esmeralda.

"Nope," she shrugged.

"I didn't know you guys were in the dog walking business too," the other kid added.

"It's a side gig," she said, making her brother almost laugh.

Once they crossed the bridge, it was a short walk up a dirt hill, and then not far from there. As they marched up the incline, Atticus noticed his shoes were caked with dirt. That should've been the first warning.

Maxwell stopped in his tracks. His back straightened as his ears raised. About ten feet in front of them, something small shifted in the dirt. First kicking sand out. A furry tail twitching. Then lifting its own head to observe who was watching it.

And that's when Maxwell bolted to chase after the squirrel.

"Maxwell, NO!" shouted Esmeralda.

As she ran after the dog, Atticus trailed behind her. A few biscuits falling out of his pockets as he struggled to keep up.

"I knew we should've brought a leash," he said, even though she couldn't hear him.

The squirrel darted in and out of the many holes it had dug in the dirt. Underground tunnels too small for a dog to get into. But that didn't stop Maxwell from trying. He stuffed his muzzle as far into them as he could, pulled out, shook off the dirt, and sneezed. And each time, the squirrel appeared in a different hole to help encourage the chase.

Maxwell pounced on one hole, caving it in, causing the squirrel to pop out the other side and begin running across the dirt field. Without any trees in the area, and out of holes, there wasn't anywhere for it to go. This allowed Maxwell time to close the distance on it. But the squirrel was slightly quicker and more dexterous as it zigzagged across the field to extend its lead.

Once out of the field, they were now close to the town square. Atticus noticed they had gotten the attention of other squirrels in the area. Some stood still on the lawn and others stopped running across the electrical wires up above. A few watched from the branches of a birch tree. But all of them were on high alert as they waved and snapped their tails to warn the others that a dog was approaching.

Not waiting for the signal, the squirrel ran across the road with Maxwell in pursuit. Thankfully an observant car slammed on its brakes and honked its horn, narrowly missing them in the process. As Atticus waved sorry, Esmeralda continued to follow after the dog.

Now in the center of town square, the squirrel ran past the city founder's statue and across the green lawn. A man seated at a park bench feeding the pigeons noticed them and gave out a hoot of encouragement to Maxwell. "You get those pesky squirrels and show 'em what for!" Maxwell barreled past him, jumping up on the park bench and leaping over it as he continued the chase.

Every squirrel on the lawn began to scatter in all directions. It almost caused Maxwell to skid to a stop, as if to decide which one to go after. But he continued after his original target. He chased it all the way up a maple tree. The squirrel used its claws to shamble up the trunk in a corkscrew pattern until it arrived at a branch out of reach. Then it watched and waited as Maxwell paced at the bottom, whining.

When the twins finally arrived, Maxwell was seated on the grass at the base of the tree, waiting for them as if nothing had happened.

"I think I have an idea . . . how Maxwell got lost . . . in the first place," said Atticus while catching his breath.

"Well that was fun," Esmeralda approved as she scratched Maxwell behind his ears. "You really should give him something to eat though."

Atticus reached into his pockets and realized all his biscuits had tumbled out during the chase. He gave his sister a look of exasperation.

They found their way back to where they were originally headed, using neighborhood sidewalks while avoiding any further areas that could become trouble spots for things to chase. And they walked up the path to the front door of the Mordred house, ready to return Maxwell to his home.

CHAPTER 8

After leading them here, Maxwell sat proudly in front of the strange structure in the Mordred house.

A large obelisk loomed before them.

"It kind of looks like a grandfather clock," noticed Atticus.

"Not any grandfather I know," said his sister.

It was very tall and made from stone. Possibly granite. With two closed vertical panels leading up to a round clock face. There were four curved "hands" on its dial with a unique twisted design, but no numbers or Roman numerals of any legible kind. And it was surprisingly smooth in the front and cold to the touch. It was definitely not like anything they'd seen before.

Atticus stood on his tip toes, staring up, to try to get a closer look.

"What time is it?" asked Esmeralda.

"I'm not sure it tells time," answered Atticus.

"Maybe it just needs to be wound up," she offered.

"I don't think you should touch that thing," warned Atticus. "We don't know what it might do."

Taller than her brother and able to reach the arms, Esmeralda began to turn them in clockwise fashion. The rotation of its gears made a clicking sound.

Maxwell now faced the clock. He raised one paw to press against the front of it. And when he touched it, the two vertical panels opened out like doors, to reveal a hidden compartment inside.

With its stone doors open wide, Atticus stared into it. Hesitant. While his feet remained firm and unmoving.

Using his thick neck and strong nose, Maxwell

nudged the twins forward to enter the clock. It was large enough to accommodate all three of them, so they entered inside of it together.

"Why are we in here?" asked Atticus, starting to panic.

"I blame the dog," she said with a grin.

Without warning, the stone doors closed shut behind them, leaving them in darkness. Atticus reached out to try to push the doorway open, but couldn't touch it. Or any of their surroundings. Whatever they were inside now apparently didn't have walls anymore. But the darkness was getting to him, even after his sister put her arm around him.

"Breathe, Atty. It's okay. We're right here with you," assured Esmeralda.

"But where is *here*, exactly?!" Atticus cried.

"Use your flashlight," Esmeralda recommended.

"I—I—didn't bring one!" stammered Atticus.

He could feel her shaking her head in the darkness next to him. "So unlike you, little brother."

The floor beneath them hummed.

"Do you feel that?" asked Atticus. "I think we're moving."

"It feels like an elevator," she guessed, making her brother gulp in dread. "Except we're not going up or down. It kinda feels like we're shifting sideways."

Maxwell barked in agreement.

Suddenly the darkness around them was getting brighter. A bright light was racing toward them that couldn't be avoided. The twins passed through it and fell into . . .

. . . somewhere . . .

CHAPTER 2

The twins felt an immediate sense of weightlessness as their bodies hovered in the white light of space. For this moment, there wasn't any ground beneath them, any walls around them, or any ceiling above them. It was all the more confusing as they felt stationary while also speeding toward something they were unable to see.

It also made Atticus feel very ill, considering he already had a weak stomach. *I think I'm going to throw up.*

"Hold it together, Atty. This is too exciting to miss

out on!" Esmeralda told him as her body tumbled in the white light.

Maxwell was the only one who seemed perfectly calm. His ears flapping above him and his feet dangling beneath him, without a care in the world.

The light around them suddenly turned into a kaleidoscope of swirling colors. A painter's wheel of hues that spun while trying to decide what to settle on. It slowed down enough to come into focus as they flew through an open doorway and into another world.

They fell out of an open portal to the ground. A second later, Atticus threw up all over the patch of grass they landed on. As he wiped his mouth, he looked back at his sister to apologize, but she was already standing and taking in their surroundings.

"This . . . is . . . COOL!" exclaimed Esmeralda.

Atticus gingerly stood up to join her, with his mouth slightly ajar. It was literally like their whole world was turned on its side.

Giant oak, elm, cedar, and redwood trees grew parallel to the ground, stretching horizontally across. The mountainous terrain in the distance was also tilted and extending outward instead of upward. Bushes and rock formations, hills and valleys—all were sideways in appearance. Even the clouds looked like they were falling off the sky.

It was almost too much to accept, and Atticus's stomach grew unsettled again. The low atmosphere, the topsy-turviness of it all, was making him stay nauseous. But he didn't have long to dwell on those feelings as his sister was already off and running.

"Esmeralda . . . wait . . . where are you going?" he shouted as she immediately ran toward the nearest tree.

"Check this out, little brother!" she hollered back.

Esmeralda had a habit of running, climbing, and jumping off everything. It started with the roof to their home when she was a few years old. She managed to climb up the drainage pipe, crawl across the shingled roof, and dive off the highest point, landing in the shrubs below. And it only got worse from there. She climbed the tree in the backyard and climbed over to the neighbor's trees as well. She found an old eucalyptus tree at school and scrambled up the side of it, across all the branches, and hopped over the fence, leaving a mess of shredded bark in her wake. And even on a dare, only to herself, she managed to climb to the top of the city water tower for fun.

So it was no shock that the first thing she would do in this crazy new world would be to climb something. It just happened to be a large tree growing sideways. With her hands wrapped around the trunk and using the branches like gym bars in the sandbox, she hung from it and kept climbing higher and higher, eventually landing on the ground where she'd started. She looked back at her brother and raised her arms in victory.

"I think I'm going to like this place," said Esmeralda.

But all Atticus could think of was that the Mordreds' clock was unlike any clock he had seen before. Much like the place it had transported them to.

CHAPTER 9

"I can't believe I'm saying this, but . . .
WAIT UP!" yelled Esmeralda.

Atticus ran out the front door of the Mordred
house, leaving it open behind him. And he hurried
home, as fast as his legs would carry him, as
Esmeralda trailed behind him the whole way.

Once inside the house, he locked and double-locked
all the doors. Made sure all the windows were closed.
Drew all the blinds shut. And began pacing around the
kitchen in a panic. It wasn't until Esmeralda opened
the fridge and offered him something that he paused.

"In case of emergency, tear here," she said, handing him a chocolate cupcake package. The kind with the swirly frosting on top. His favorite.

"Where did you get this?" he asked with cheeks full of sugar.

"I stashed away some extras for situations like this," she replied. "You looked like you could use it."

Atticus sat down at the kitchen counter long enough to catch his breath. But his mind was racing a mile a minute. He rattled off a bunch of questions out loud. *"Where was that weird place we went to? What exactly is that strange looking clock? Why do the Mordreds have it? And what the heck was that scary creature that tried to eat us?"*

Esmeralda shrugged. She was the type who seemed content not knowing all the answers. But happy for the experience.

"Maybe you should take your mind off it. Maybe do some homework," she offered.

"Homework can wait," he said. "This is more important!"

Now she knew he was distressed. Atticus wasn't the type to turn down schoolwork lightly. But she knew better than to get in his way at this point. She excused herself to her bedroom to allow her brother the space he'd need to get to the bottom of things.

He went to the den. Hung the DO NOT DISTURB sign on the outside door. And closed it behind him. Atticus didn't come out for the rest of the evening.

After distracting herself with various activities around the house, Esmeralda felt she was running out of options. So she fixed herself a steaming hot chicken potpie for dinner. And then used it as an excuse to see what her brother was doing.

Carrying a tray of food to him, she waited outside the den, and then knocked. Pressing her ear against the door, she didn't hear any reaction. After knocking one more time, she opened the door and let herself in. And that's when she found him, using a leaning stack of books as a pillow and his arms folded underneath his head. Atticus had fallen asleep at his desk. Scattered around him were scientific diagrams and open encyclopedias for researching clocks, physics, and reptiles.

Esmeralda smiled at him from the open doorway. The poor thing had worried and studied himself to sleep. Leaving it up to her to get him to bed. A task she was all too familiar with.

Lifting his body and wrapping his arms around her neck, she carried him piggyback style up the staircase, down the hall, and into his bedroom. Then she gently lowered him onto his mattress. She removed his shoes, left him in his school clothes, and tucked him in with his blanket. She went to turn off his bedroom light on the way out, but a tired voice stopped her.

"What happened today?" Atticus asked sleepily with his eyes closed.

"We had an adventure," she answered.

After a short pause, causing her to think he had fallen asleep, he continued. "Let's not do that again," he said while dozing off.

"Too late," she replied. "That's just part of being in this family."

As he quietly snored, she left his door slightly open, and she ventured back to the kitchen to finish her dinner.

✹   ✹   ✹

In the darkness, Atticus had trouble sensing his surroundings. But as his eyes adjusted, he could make out a familiar texture in the ceiling. He was back home, in his room, lying in bed. His blankets were tangled around him. His pillow on the floor.

Everything that happened at the Mordred's house, inside the clock, and sideways across to that mystical place . . . Did he just dream it all? Unsure, he stared at the ceiling for clarity. Unlike most dreams, this one hadn't faded from memory. It was all too real.

Sliding into some soft fuzzy slippers, Atticus began to shuffle down the hallway of his home. He could sense it was still early in the morning, but the kitchen was loud as he approached.

Rubbing his eyes, Atticus asked, "Mom? Dad? Are you home?"

"Nope. Chef 'Ralda at your service!" beamed his sister, uncommonly awake and happy at this hour.

Eggs were scrambling in a pan on the stove, while their shells were cracked all over the kitchen floor. Bacon sizzled in the fryer next to it. Three pieces, extra crispy, how he liked it. And three others extra rubbery for her. As if on cue, the toast sprung out of the toaster onto a plate on the counter. A choice of butter, jelly, or cinnamon sugar waited to be decided upon. And on the table was a pitcher of juice that merged three of the best fruits together . . . orange, pineapple, and banana.

It was a breakfast spread fit for a king. Or at least a little brother who had been through the ringer these past couple days.

"Okay, this must be a dream. I've never seen you cook," observed Atticus.

"Of course I can cook. It's just easier to let you do it," she smiled.

He bit into the bacon with closed eyes and a wide smile as it crunched in his mouth, followed by the fluffy but runny taste of eggs. Yeah . . . this was definitely a dream.

They both chewed in silence across from each other. He waited until they both finished their plates to thank her. But mainly so he wouldn't ruin their morning, before he was ready to start their next conversation.

"Are we going to talk about what happened yesterday?" asked Atticus with some hesitation.

"I'll admit, that was a pretty cool place to go see," she remembered.

"Cool?!" Atticus exclaimed. "That thing tried to eat us! And burn us!"

Esmeralda gathered up the dirty plates off the table. "And here you got breakfast out of the deal. Win-win if you ask me."

"I don't know . . ." he said, trailing off in thought.

"Put your brain on pause," she recommended. "Because we've got to hotfoot it to school. We're already late."

"WHAT?!" Atticus looked at his wristwatch. She was right. "Why didn't you warn me?"

"And ruin my fantastic breakfast? No way! But don't worry. It's only school," she explained.

Now it was Atticus grabbing his sister by the wrist as they ran out the front door. It was a twenty-minute walk to school from their house. But they could probably make it in ten if they ran, which they did. But Atticus made it in fifteen. His sister was always the better athlete.

The hallways inside Thorns Academy were empty and freshly waxed. Apparently the janitor was the only one who had been by here recently. All the students were already in their classrooms.

"With great sorrow, we must depart," Esmeralda said in dramatic fashion. "See you after detention, little brother!" And with that, she skipped down the hallway to her class.

Now alone, Atticus was trying to think up the perfect excuse for being late. He had so many chambered in his mind, but realized he'd used all of them before. Out sick. Out of town. At the doctors. Even this gem . . . the dog ate my homework, which is one of the few realistic drawbacks in his line of work.

But he realized he had no good excuse. At least, not one that he was willing to share aloud.

"Another sick day, Mister Fetch?" questioned Miss Grobber as Atticus entered his full classroom.

"No, ma'am," he responded.

"Very well. Take a seat in the corner and face the wall as punishment for being tardy."

As he walked past the students, he was met with laughter, spitballs, and an outstretched foot that tried to trip him. But he couldn't be bothered to fall. He found an open desk in the back, faced the wall, and stared. At least this could allow his mind to wander just like his ceiling back home. A "punishment" he'd gladly accept.

There were posters on the wall encouraging academic achievement. Some with crude drawings to pass as art. And mathematical pie charts. But none of those were as interesting as the smoke that Atticus noticed starting to filter in through the vent along the ceiling.

He waved his hand to get the teacher's attention to warn about the smoke, but she ignored him. Even under threat of detention, he broke his silence.

"Miss Grobber!" Atticus yelled, "There's smoke coming out of the vents! I think the school is on fire!"

She stopped in the middle of her lesson, adjusted her glasses, and squinted at the smoke coming from the vent.

"I'm not sure I entirely believe you, Mister Fetch."

"Fine then, don't. I'll go find someone who does," he stated as he ran out of the classroom.

He entered a hallway filled with thick plumes of smoke everywhere. Visibility was extremely low.

The only thing he was able to see was the tiled floor and the hint of lockers surrounding them.

Atticus cautiously walked through the clouds of smoke, having pulled his shirt up over his nose to try to breathe easier. It helped a little, but he still found it hard to breathe and began to cough. It was then that he was grabbed from behind, with a hand covering his mouth.

"*Ssssh . . . keep quiet,*" she warned.

It was Esmeralda who found him in the smoke With a finger over her mouth, and her other hand pointing into the smoke clouds, they crouched low to the ground and didn't move. They stayed this way for a minute until something else passed close by. Something with scaly skin, an elongated body, and heat emanating from its sharp open mouth.

It was slithering through the hallways, in and out of classrooms, methodically looking for something. Or a pair of someones.

The mythical creature from the clock at the Mordred house had followed them to their school.

Unable to hold his breath any further, and with his lungs starting to fill with smoke, Atticus exhaled and let out a cough. And gave away their position to the giant reptile. It darted toward them at a frenetic speed, parting the smoke clouds in the process.

"Run, Atty!" Esmeralda shouted. And for the first time, Atticus beat his sister in a race.

He ran around the corner and found an empty classroom to duck into. Esmeralda was right behind him as she closed the classroom door shut. In the darkness, they crawled along the ground and found hiding spots among the desks.

And just in time since the reptile was able to open the door to follow them inside.

The room remained dark aside from an eerie orange glow coming from inside the reptile's mouth. Bursts of flame exhaust would pop from its mouth as it slithered between the desks. It stopped each time to arch its neck and taste the air, trying to locate them by smell.

Now pointed in their direction, they didn't wait to be caught. Esmeralda scooped up her brother onto her back to carry him, and ran across the floor. But her boots squeaked on the freshly waxed tile, alerting the reptile that its prey was making their escape.

As she opened the door, the reptile was already on top of them. Its jaw locked onto Atticus' shoe, trying to pull him off his sister's back. But Atticus had a tight grip and wouldn't let go. Each side tugging, but the twins were starting to lose ground.

"Grab the door frame," she ordered her brother, releasing him from her back.

"Don't leave me!" Atticus pleaded, desperately grabbing the frame tightly as the reptile continued to tug.

"Never! I've got an idea," she said as she charged out into the hallway of smoke.

Atticus could barely make out his sister who became enveloped in the dark smoke, even as he was concentrating to hold onto the door. But then he noticed her across the hall near the wall. Followed by a shrill sound.

RRRRRRRRRUUUUUUNNNNNGGGGGGGGG

Esmeralda first pulled the fire alarm. Then removed an item next to it. A small hand axe attached to the wall.

"Yes—hit it!" Atticus shouted. And when she returned, she swung for the reptile's head. The blade wasn't sharp enough, or its scales were too protected, because the axe didn't cut or hurt it.

With Atticus losing his grip, he corrected himself. "Don't hit it with that! Go back and hit the glass and bring that over! *Hurry!!*"

Returning to the wall where she grabbed it from, she used the axe to break open the container next to the alarm. Inside was a fire extinguisher. Discarding the axe on the ground, she carried the canister back toward her brother, and pointed its nozzle at the creature. The white retardant fluid sprayed into its eyes and foamed on the ground around them.

The reptile released his leg from its mouth. Its long body convulsing as it curled and twisted on the floor in agony. But it stopped long enough to retreat to a far window in the classroom, and lunge through it, breaking the glass as it scurried off to escape into the woods.

As Esmeralda helped her scared brother off the floor, someone else stood next to them. As the smoke cleared, they recognized the curly haired head of classmate Stevie Sweeney. His jaw was wide-open along with his eyes. He was stunned but had one thing to ask:

"Whoa! What was that thing?!"

THE HALLOW HERALD

FREAKY FACULTY FIR[E]

School burns under scary conditions!

by Doris Dane

A fire broke out under suspicious circu[m]stances at Thorns Academy yesterday afterno[on]. Giant plumes of smoke could be seen across [the] city, rising above the tall campus buildings. A[nd] multiple fires had to be put out by the city [fire] department. Due to the immeasurable amoun[t of] damage and unsafe conditions, the school [is] currently shut down for the year, with stude[nts] and staff being sent home for an extend[ed] summer break.

There's some discrepancy ab[out] where the fire started. And how it w[as] able to spread to multiple classrooms a[nd] unconnected buildings simultaneou[sly] while leaving other areas nearby unda[m]aged. Police aren't ruling out arson, [but] explained it seems unlikely due to [the] coordination it would take to cover [the] distance required to start each fire. "[It's] almost like the fire was chasing som[e]one from one area to the next while picking and choosing where to attack," said the chief of police. "But it's kind of a preposterous theory."

Most of the young students were unreachable or too afraid to comment. But one was willing to share his thoughts.

"I think it was a dragon. Or a fire-breathing snake!" said excited student Stevie Sweeney. "It was kind of hard to see it in the smoke and flames, but it was totally stalking us. I swear! Also I believe there are trolls in the cafeteria. They ate my lunch yesterday."

Asked to comment, the police chief only offered the following, "It's obvious this was a stressful incident that scared everyone at this school. But reports of a monster are highly exaggerated."

The public school board stands behind the police chief's comments. "This appears to be an unfortunate electrical accident" is their official statement at this time.

We tried to reach out to multiple teachers and staff, but none have returned our calls.

OUR TRIP IS ALMOST WRAPPED UP. WE'VE SEEN A LOT OF SIGHTS AND HAVE BEEN ABLE TO GATHER SOME GREAT PIECES FOR THE MUSEUM EXHIBIT ON LOAN FROM THE REGION. ANOTHER SUCCESSFUL TRIP!

BUT WHAT'S THIS I HEAR ABOUT YOUR SCHOOL CATCHING FIRE? PLEASE TELL ME THAT YOU'RE OKAY. ALSO THAT NEITHER OF YOU ARE RESPONSIBLE FOR IT. I CAN'T HELP BUT WORRY SINCE I'M NOT THERE TO SEE FOR MYSELF. BUT I WILL BE SOON.

— MOM

PERU

P.S. KOPI SAYS HELLO!

CHAPTER 10

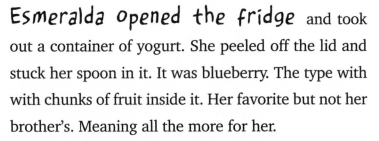

Esmeralda opened the fridge and took out a container of yogurt. She peeled off the lid and stuck her spoon in it. It was blueberry. The type with with chunks of fruit inside it. Her favorite but not her brother's. Meaning all the more for her.

She skipped over to the kitchen table where Atticus sat there moping. "Why aren't you more excited, Atty? It's early summer vacation!" she cheered.

"And why aren't you more scared? That creature tried to eat me!!" exclaimed her brother.

She continued sticking spoonfuls of yogurt into her mouth, unaffected.

"Yeah, that wasn't great. But at least we got something out of it. No school for awhile," she added.

Atticus sunk his head into his hands. Things were going from weird, to bad, to worse very quickly lately. And it all pointed back to the Mordreds. He felt responsible for that creature following them to school and burning it. They were lucky that no one was hurt.

"If we never went to the Mordreds in the first place, then none of this would've happened," whined Atticus.

Esmeralda corrected him. "And if we never cleaned the basement, then none of this would've happened either. Lesson learned. Never clean things. Or just blame Dad."

That last line made Atticus crack half a smile. Esmeralda was satisfied to get that much out of him.

"While you mope in here, I'll grab the mail," she offered.

She placed her carton of yogurt on the table as she walked out the front door. Atticus reached for her yogurt, thinking he might finish it. Until he saw the chunks. And realized that's a line even he wouldn't cross. He stuck out his tongue in disgust.

"Atty! Come outside and see this," she yelled.

Atticus sprung up from the kitchen table. He was already on edge and now was expecting any kind of danger outside. But when he joined her, it was something else entirely.

Esmeralda was standing by the mailbox, which was overflowing with letters and notes. It was fully overstuffed, with more envelopes that had fallen onto the ground.

"Help me get all these inside," asked Esmeralda.

She scooped up two armfuls and marched to the kitchen. Atticus did the same and followed her inside, being careful not to drop any along the way. They dumped them into a pile on the kitchen table.

Atticus sifted through the pile, quickly glancing at each as he started to separate the pile.

"Where are all these from?" Esmeralda asked.

"Here in town," he replied. "Notes and letters from everyone with missing pets around the city!"

"So business is booming! We need to put out a want ad and hire more staff," she joked.

"It's obvious what is responsible for scaring these pets away. Or worse . . ." he implied, thinking some might've been eaten by the creature they encountered at school that escaped.

"What are we going to do?" asked Esmeralda.

Atticus had only one answer. His favorite answer. "Research!"

They took the bus and arrived at the university that afternoon. As the children of a university professor, they'd been granted free access to its vast library. And were always welcomed and recognized when they came to use it.

"Ahhh, young mister Fetch and sister Fetch. A pleasure to see you both today," greeted the university librarian. She was a thin elderly lady with a keen eye and sharp wit. And enjoyed their company.

"Hello Gladys. How have you been?" inquired Atticus.

"Busy. Spring is upon us, so we've had a lot of students cramming for finals. Our supply might be low, so I hope we still have any books that you're looking for."

"I'm sure I'll find something," he assured her.

"You always do," she retorted.

Atticus knew the layout well. Periodicals near the couches and sleeping students, the nonfiction section on one side, fiction on the other, alphabetical and broken down into sections. Science, philosophy, history . . . just about any scholarly subject. But he'd be trying a new section. One he was less familiar with and hoped they had what he needed.

After taking the stairs, he wandered to a darkened area of the library on the third floor. Past the students sitting in cramped alcoves studying by lamplight. Past the statue busts of famous authors and historians. And to a more dusty unused section of books. A few long ladders on wheels were attached to the shelving here. And as he stared sideways at the spine of each book as he looked, his sister had already commandeered a ladder and rolled toward him. Its wheels screeching along the floor.

"Look out, Atty. Coming through!" she hollered, narrowly missing her brother, who sidestepped to avoid being run over at the last possible second.

As he resumed his search, he stopped at the section

he was looking for. There weren't a lot of books in this area, but there were enough. His fingers ran along the top of each book as he determined which he'd need. When Esmeralda rejoined him, he began handing her a carefully selected stack to help him carry.

She let out a donkey whinny. "Book mule at your service," she said.

"Giddyup, let's go!" he replied, to play along.

They arrived back at the front desk, placing the stack of books on top for checkout.

"I'll put this on your tab, young mister Fetch," she offered.

As she catalogued what he was taking, she couldn't help but notice the types of books he was checking out. All of them from their folklore and mythology section. She lowered her glasses, lowered her shoulders, and leaned over the counter so only they could hear.

"It might be of interest to you to check out our *Wierd Wall* over there," she pointed.

Aside from want ads, signups for fraternities and sororities, and a list for students looking for roommates, the board had a curio section with some interesting newspaper and magazine clippings all posted together.

Atticus and Esmeralda stared at the Wierd Wall and realized that Thorns Hollow might be home to more than just people with friendly pets.

"What is all of this? Some kind of college prank I bet," guessed Esmeralda as she looked at the bulletin board of strange creatures.

"I don't think so," surmised Atticus as he rubbed his chin. "There have been other mythical monster sightings from the looks of it. But I don't see the one that followed us to school."

"There's a monster at your school?" asked the eavesdropping librarian, now standing behind them. "Well now, isn't that peculiar."

"No . . . I mean . . . it's nothing, really. Just kids and their wild imaginations," stammered Atticus, trying to keep it a secret.

"You should have seen him run from his *imagination*," added Esmeralda. "He's pretty fast when he needs to be. A giant snake monster chasing you will do that!"

Atticus shot Esmeralda a sideways glance of

disapproval. But his sister just ignored him.

Gladys stood between them to pin up a new article to the bulletin board. This one featured a blurry photo of what appeared to be a three-headed hydra.

"Clearly this one's a fake," Gladys pondered. "Hydras usually have more heads, from the ones I've seen. Unless, of course, this one hasn't regenerated yet."

The librarian began to casually walk away, pushing a squeaky cart of books around the corner and out of sight. Atticus and Esmeralda exchanged a curious look with each other, and then quickly followed after her.

The book cart was left abandoned next to a private study room. The room's door left suspiciously ajar. The twins approached it with caution, while a soft voice beckoned them from inside the room.

"Come inside and close the door behind you," said Gladys.

These nondescript soundproof rooms with plain white walls were here for students to quietly study. Instead, the librarian sat across the empty table waiting for them to take a seat. The twins each pulled out a chair and sat down.

"You've seen a hydra? Actually seen one?" asked Atticus in disbelief.

Gladys adjusted her thin-framed glasses, sliding them down the bridge of her nose so her eyes peeked at them from over the rims. "*Maybe,*" she answered with her voice trailing away. "Or maybe that's not all I've seen."

Esmeralda couldn't contain herself. Her nose snorted while trying to stifle a laugh.

Gladys cocked an eyebrow. "You don't believe me? When have I ever lied to you two?"

The twins couldn't think of any situation from before. After they shook their heads in silence, she continued.

"I'm not saying all those articles on that wall are the real deal. But some of them certainly are," said Gladys. "I've lived in this town for most of my life and I've had a few, let's call them *encounters*, myself."

Atticus leaned forward. "Like what?"

"I used to collect fairies as a child. Any that I could find in the vegetable garden behind my house. Pressed them into a book even," answered Gladys. "Of course, I lost that book. Lost most things from my youth, as childhoods go."

"Maybe it was just a fallen leaf from a tree that you found and placed in your book," guessed Esmeralda. "It's probably easy to confuse the two."

"Leaves don't have wings attached to tiny human bodies," corrected Gladys. "That wasn't all. There was the water spirit with the horse head that sometimes appeared at the lake during our summer trips."

"I've heard of that one," confirmed Atticus. "A kelpie!"

"Some thought it was just a drowned park ranger's horse who wandered off the hiking trail. A silly campfire story," continued Gladys. "Only this horse had fins. And if you were lucky, you might catch a glimpse of its giant fish tail breaching the water to slap the lake in the moonlight."

"We need to go camping!" encouraged Esmeralda to her brother.

"Just be careful, you two," warned Gladys as she stood up to the leave the room. "And make sure you return those books you've checked out after two weeks. Or that giant snake monster will be the least of your worries!"

CHAPTER 11

The Fetch twins spent the rest of their evening back home in their kitchen. It was the central focal point of the house and the easiest place to spread things out to study. But even more important was its proximity to acquiring desserts. An infinite amount of chocolate cake or scoops of malted ice cream have been consumed here in the name of "research." And it would be no different tonight.

Esmeralda licked her rainbow-colored icicle pop as she watched her brother in action. With discarded snack cake wrappers around him, there were multiple books spread out on the table. Chapters analyzed. Notes being written.

After he found one specific section, he held the book close so he could read it aloud . . .

The basilisk or "serpent king" is a legendary reptile believed hatched by a rooster from the egg of a serpent or toad. The earliest account of one described was in roughly 79 AD from Medieval Europe, but also hints at Egyptian and biblical ancestry. Known for its elongated body with features of both snake and lizard in some cases, with toxic poisonous breath, and whose single gaze can cause death. Also with a venomous bite and an ability to breathe fire. Its only weakness is the odor of the weasel.

"Maybe you're alive because you still stink from that ferret Elbo we found earlier," thought Esmeralda.

"I'm not sure if that counts," responded Atticus. "But this sure sounds like that creature that followed us to school!"

Satisfied by finding its description in a textbook, Atticus slumped back in his chair. He let out a silent yawn he held for a few seconds.

"Yeah . . . watching you read books makes me tired as well," she playfully interjected.

"It's late. We can resume again tomorrow," said Atticus, leaving everything in the kitchen. "Although I'm not sure if I'll be able to get any sleep, knowing that creature is still loose out there."

"Don't worry, little brother. I'll protect you. I've got a mean stare all my own," she offered, making a face so he'd laugh. "And since there's no school, you finally get to experience what I normally do everyday. Sleeping in!"

"Good night, Es. And thanks for saving me today. Thanks for always looking out for me," he said sincerely.

"That's what a big sister is for," she replied as she walked down the hallway to her bedroom.

Atticus put on his pajamas and slipped under the sheets to his bed. The room was dark and quiet. The ceiling waiting for him to stare before falling asleep. And there was some comfort in being home with his sister nearby.

And much sooner than expected, within minutes, he was snoring peacefully.

Time passes strangely at night as one passes in and out of their sleep cycle. Minutes can feel like hours, and hours like minutes. Or maybe it was all the sugar in his system making him restless. But it didn't feel like he had been asleep for more than a few hours before he was awakened by a sudden noise coming from inside his room. Whatever made it stood in the open doorway to his bedroom. The one he had previously shut before heading to sleep.

He tumbled out of bed, half awake, grabbing for the closest thing nearby that he could use to defend himself . . . a spelling bee trophy he had been awarded. It wasn't even made of metal, so he doubted it could do much damage, but it was the only thing that found his hand in the darkness.

"You can put that down unless you plan on fighting us with words," said his sister. "Of course you would. You're a spelling champion."

Atticus was relieved to know it was Esmeralda and he dropped the trophy to the floor. "Not really. I got second place."

He realized she wasn't alone. Standing next to her, wagging his tail in the dark hallway, was Maxwell.

"Yeah he came to my window tonight and pawed at it until I let him in," she said. "He made a convincing argument."

"What's that in his mouth?" Atticus asked.

Maxwell held a small book in his jaw. It felt like Esmeralda was noticing it for the first time as well.

She scratched Maxwell behind the ear, finding the exact spot that activated his leg to *thump thump thump* on the ground. By doing so, his grip loosened and he released the book into her other hand.

The cover to the small book only had one word on the cover: DIARY.

And inside the opening page it said PROPERTY OF MELANIE.

Atticus took the book from his sister and began to open it up, much to her shock.

"What do you think you're doing?" she asked with a tone to her voice.

"It must be important if Maxwell brought it to us," he theorized.

"That doesn't mean you should read it. It's a girl's private diary! That's sacred," she insisted. "It's not meant for anyone but her, whomever she is."

He took a moment to think it over before agreeing. Atticus closed the book shut.

But Maxwell had other ideas. With a bark and thrusting his paw out, he knocked the book out of Atty's hands. It landed on the floor, faceup, and open to a handwritten passage.

"So it wasn't by accident that Maxwell opened that stone clock that we went inside of," observed Atticus.

"Or that he brought this diary to us," continued Esmeralda. "He's a pretty smart dog."

The twins looked over at Maxwell, impressed by his actions. Maxwell lowered his head to rest it on the floor and closed his eyes. Not to sleep, but to acknowledge they were finally paying attention. His lips even curled upwards on his muzzle as if to smile. Esmeralda immediately turned the page to the next entry.

"Hey! What are you doing?" asked Atticus, a little perturbed at his sister.

She looked back at him with the most puzzled, innocent look on her face. "We've got to read more!"

"But what about this diary being private and sacred?" asked Atticus. Now she was sounding hypocritical.

"You didn't really believe all that, did you?" she sighed. "Oh you've got so much to learn, little brother. Besides, we've already started to read it. We can't just stop now."

"Like when you climbed up that pine tree in the forest?" recalled Atticus. "And Mom and Dad yelled at you to come down, but you kept climbing anyways. Then fell, hitting all the branches on the way down."

"Those pine needles helped break my fall," bragged Esmeralda.

"*I* helped break your fall," frowned Atticus. "And *you* helped break my back."

"Heh . . . yeah," remembered Esmeralda with a grin. Then she turned the question back toward her brother. "But when's the last time you ever snuck into the pantry, opened a box of choco-crunch, and didn't stop until you finished?"

Atticus sat there silently not wanting to answer. He hated to admit she was right.

"Fine. You made your case," he said begrudgingly. "I guess it couldn't hurt to keep reading at this point."

Esmeralda's eyes lit up. "And maybe there's even more secrets to find out!"

As Esmeralda continued to read aloud, Atticus could feel his head starting to bob. His eyes were growing heavy. At this late hour it was becoming hard to stay focused, so he laid back, resting his head against Maxwell, who didn't seem to mind.

Eventually his sister's words began to trail off, growing more and more quiet, until the only sound in the room was a quiet ripple of snores. Any secrets would have to wait.

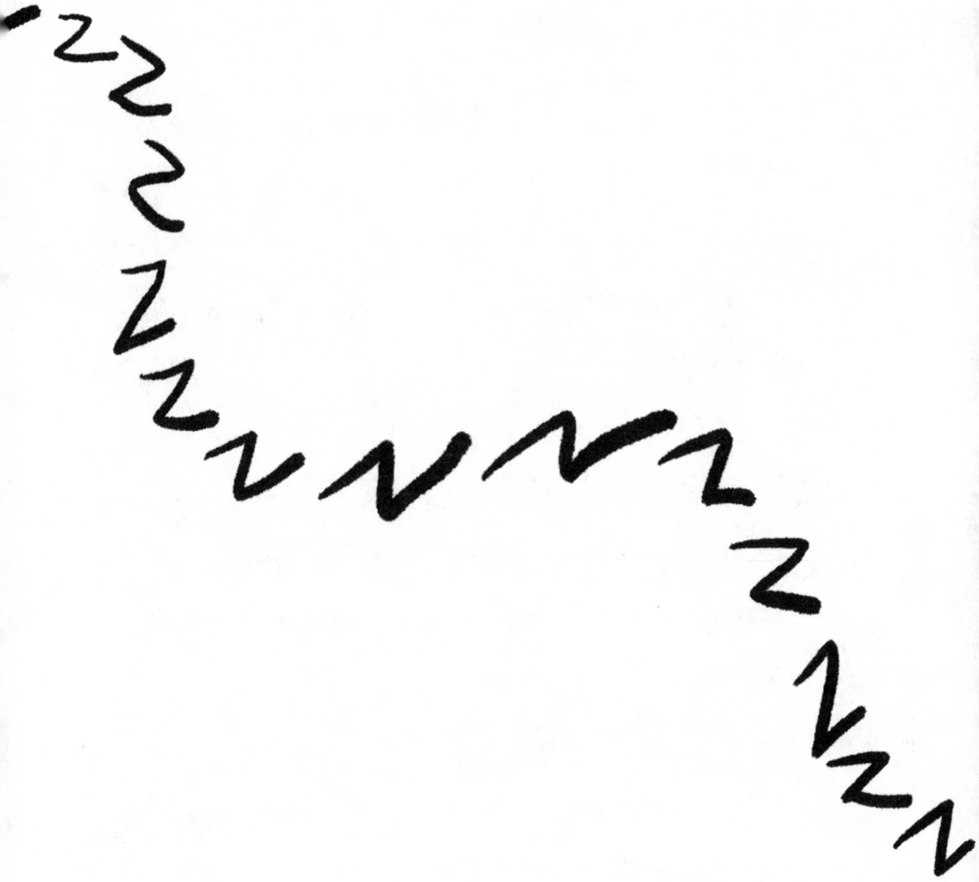
ZZZZZZZZZZZZZ

Mum and dad have left on a field trip again. That's the third time this week.

They're never gone for very long. And they always seem to do it when I've set down for an afternoon nap. I think so they can sneak away without me knowing. But I just pretend that I'm asleep. I'm actually awake the entire time, listening as the house gets quiet when they vanish away.

My only company is Maxwell. And he's good company too. Never leaves my side and a very warm body to sleep on. And when he dreams, his cheek flaps quiver and buzz. I can't help but giggle. But it sometimes wakes him up with the most confused look on his face.

I wish they'd take me wherever they go. It's got to be more fun than being stuck in this creaky old house. I've promised to stay quiet and out of the way. But every time I ask, they say it's for work. And I'm not allowed.

Not allowed? What do they even mean by that?

I think even Maxwell is curious where they go. Lately he's been following them downstairs when they leave. If he finds out, I hope he tells me. Or better yet . . . shows me.

CHAPTER 12

The next morning, they found themselves piled together on the floor of Atty's room. Maxwell's large, heated body curled around the twins, keeping them warm as they slept. The diary was still open at the page they left off.

Atticus was the first awake. Trying not to make any sudden movement, he slowly reached across and tapped his sister awake. But as he shifted, it woke Maxwell up as well. His big brown eyes looked at Atty, then felt Esmeralda close by, and feeling content, he closed his eyes again.

Eventually they did wake up. And knew what they had to do. Return Maxwell back to the Mordreds.

A quick breakfast for all three, and they hit the road. They strolled across town and down neighborhood sidewalks. Until they reached their dead-end destination of the Mordred house. It still looked vacant with no signs of life. And it very well could be, if the Mordreds weren't back from their field trip.

Atticus still wanted to knock anyways. It was the polite thing to do. But Maxwell brushed by him with a huffing sigh, nudging the front door open. They followed him inside.

Instead of retracing their steps before, they set out on a new path. Maxwell climbed the stairs to the second floor, waiting long enough for the twins to follow along. As they rounded a corner, he was gone. But a bark came from a room at the end of the hallway.

They entered into a child's bedroom. One that had a closet filled with dresses, a quilted bed with pink sheets, and a few scattered stuffed animals. Maxwell sat on top of the bed. His body stretched fully across so his deer-like legs claimed the entire mattress for himself. He lifted his head up slowly to watch the twins enter the room. Then he laid it back down to enjoy the comfort of soft sheets.

Esmeralda sat on a leather cushioned ottoman at the base of the bed. Atticus examined a white writing desk filled with pens and paper, arts and crafts, and a music box.

An old black-and-white family photo hung over the desk inside an intricate frame. Professor Hadrick stood posed in a finely tailored suit, Doctor Persephone at his side. And seated on a chair in front of them was a young girl with light curly hair.

"I think that's Melanie," Atticus said aloud.

Maxwell barked in agreement.

"Melanie Mordred . . . their daughter," he finished.

Esmeralda turned back to face Maxwell. "If you're her dog, then where is Melanie?"

Maxwell sunk deeper into her bed with depression.

"I guess we've got our next case," said Esmeralda.

Atticus shook his head in disagreement. "Not

a good idea. We only look for lost pets. Missing kids . . . that's something different."

"Call Fetch and we'll find! Maxwell came to us with this request," reminded Esmeralda. "Besides, how can you say no to this face?" She smooshed her face up against Maxwell's cheek flaps. His brow furrowed with soft wrinkles, giving a doe-eyed look toward Atticus.

With his hands on his hips, staring at the two of them, Atticus pondered what they should do. But before he could decide, he noticed Maxwell's head perk up suddenly at attention.

A chime came from downstairs.

Leaping off the bed, Maxwell jogged out of the room. The twins hurried to catch up. As they hid at the top of the staircase out of view, they were able to see the clock obelisk activate. The clock hands turning and clicking. The stone doors shifting and opening from within.

Something was coming over from the other side . . .

CHAPTER 13

Professor Hadrick and Doctor Persephone stepped out of the clock, arriving back into their home.

They returned carrying their bags and suitcases they had previously packed, and placed them on the floor. They both stopped and waited in silence. Listening to their house for sounds, as if expecting it.

Atticus and Esmeralda held their breaths. Even though they were out of view, they didn't want the floorboards to creak or to accidentally knock something over that would alert the Mordreds they were trespassing.

With the house quietly settled and appearing normal, the Mordreds began to move again. Persephone turned to her husband and adjusted his hair. A long strand was falling down in front of his glasses, and she brushed it aside. He held her hand against his cheek as they looked at each other without speaking. Their expressions were weary. Tired from their travels. And Atticus couldn't help but notice something odd.

"Didn't they have blond hair before?" asked Atticus quietly.

"You're right! And now it's fully white on both of them. But they're not that old," she whispered back. *"That's so weird."*

Leaving their bags behind, the Mordreds moved into their study in the next room. They called out for Maxwell, expecting him to greet their return, but when the dog didn't show up, they seemed concerned. Or worse . . . suspicious.

"That dog!" exclaimed the professor with consternation, unable to locate him. "Not again."

"Honey, not now," pleaded his wife. "I'm sure he's around here somewhere."

"Maxwell? Maxwell, come here boy!" he continued to shout.

Hearing his name, Maxwell left the twins and bounded down the stairs. When he joined his family in the study, he hopped up on his back legs and swung his front paws toward Doctor Persephone. She caught them and began to dance with the dog as his furry feet shuffled along the floor. After releasing him back to all fours, she wrapped her arms around him and hugged him back.

"See, he's here. This is his way of saying he missed us," she said.

"Yeah, well, we're missing a lot of things," alluded the professor with a stern voice.

With the twins' weight pressed against the staircase railing to listen, one of the beams shifted loose. Before they could grab it, it popped off and tumbled to the floor below. As it rattled on the ground, the sound was like a thunderclap, echoing through the house.

"What was that?" asked Persephone.

"Stay here while I look," he told her. Finding the wooden piece on the floor in the next room, he picked it up. While he adjusted his glasses, he looked above where it fell from. The Fetch twins leaned back to stay out of sight.

"One of the staircase rail supports came loose," he announced. "Or maybe something knocked it out."

"Please be careful," she advised her husband.

The professor started to walk toward the base of the stairs to make his way up. The twins were trapped. Even though he hadn't seen them yet, he was coming in their direction. And he was about to block their only exit, unless they climbed higher in the house and jumped from the second or third story window. Esmeralda could probably make that jump, but not Atticus. Claustrophobia wasn't the only thing that affected him; he also had a paralyzing fear of heights.

Esmeralda jabbed her brother in his side. *"He's coming, Atty! What do we do?!"*

"I don't know," Atticus whispered back. *"I don't know!"*

If they didn't decide quickly, it wouldn't matter.

As the professor placed his foot on the bottom stair, his wife yelled at him from the kitchen. Maxwell was running to the other side of the house and barking rapidly at something. It was loud enough to make the professor stop and see what the problem was. And provide the distraction needed for the twins to get out of the house.

When they got to the bottom of the staircase, Maxwell rejoined the twins, panting proudly. And the Mordreds were nowhere to be found. Maxwell seemed overly excited as he pressed and scratched against the clock, to activate the stone doors to open. He barked for the twins to join him.

"No more hiding!" scolded Atticus, "And we can't go back in there."

Maxwell barked again, this time grabbing Atticus by his shirt to tug him closer to the open clock. Atticus reached out for his sister, who grabbed him by the arm to tug back. As Atticus fought to resist being dragged inside, the Mordreds turned the corner and spotted them. The surprised looks on their faces quickly turned to anger.

"What's the meaning of this?!" shouted the professor. "What are you two doing here?!"

With a quick yank of his neck, Maxwell dragged both the twins inside the clock. While his wife shouted, the professor ran to stop them, but it was too late. The stone doors sealed shut and the clock activated.

Within seconds, they had shifted sideways . . . into another dimension.

CHAPTER 14

The wild girl seemed to have appeared out of the bushes themselves. Her dress was tattered and fraying. Her hair was all knotted. And her feet were blistering from running barefoot. But she did not care. Only for the safety of the unicorn.

She placed her hand on top of the unicorn to soothe it. Petting its soft shoulder of fur for a calming effect. She understood the arrow hurt. And she would do everything she could to relieve its pain.

As the Fetch twins watched quietly, the wild girl

positioned one hand at rest on the upper leg of the unicorn, while the other gripped the arrow. It was lodged deep into its skin. She took in a deep breath simultaneously with the unicorn drawing breath, and then pulled out the arrow as hard as she could. It tore through the air and was flung into the shrubs.

While the unicorn bled, the wild girl applied pressure to the wound until it stopped. Its fur matted together to seal the cut. It was a temporary solution, but successful given the circumstance.

The wild girl turned to face the twins. Then realized who was with them.

"How did you find me?" she asked.

"We just fell in here," responded Atticus. "We thought you found us."

The wild girl frowned. "I wasn't talking to you." And she hugged Maxwell tightly as his tail wagged back and forth.

Another two arrows shot through the air and struck in the dirt one foot away, reminding them that they were still in great danger.

"We can talk later," the wild girl commanded. "We have to get out of here right now!"

"Okay but where?" asked Esmeralda.

The wild girl responded by leaping onto the back of the unicorn. She held out her hand to encourage them to join her.

Esmeralda didn't wait to be told. She ran and easily hopped onto the unicorn's back. Atticus paused long enough for another arrow to narrowly miss him, before it spurned him forward. He jumped toward the back of the unicorn but wasn't able to make it. Knowing this, his sister was already prepared, holding out her hand to help him climb up.

Now with the three children riding on its back, and Maxwell near its side, the unicorn let out a burst of steam from its nostrils and began to gallop away, fighting through the pain. More arrows trailed on their path behind them, but the unicorn was fast enough to outpace and outdistance them. Maxwell also kept up.

Eventually the arrows stopped but they could hear the bellowing roar in the distance. It sent a chill down Atty's back as that creature was unlike any he'd ever seen. It had the head and body of a lion, giant leathery dragon-like wings, and a menacing scorpion's tail. How could it exist? How could any of this?

The unicorn picked up speed as it ran through the sideways terrain. Trees awkwardly growing and stretching out horizontally made for a unique obstacle. Yet the unicorn wasn't fazed as it leapt over their trunks, two or three at a time, without breaking speed. And it weaved around any rocky outcroppings that appeared in its way.

It instinctively came to a stop. Its ears perked up to listen. Its eyes darting around trying to catch sight of its pursuer. And the twins grew impatient.

"What are we waiting for? Let's get out of here!" urged Atticus.

"Yeah, why aren't we running?" asked Esmeralda.

"Quiet!" commanded the wild girl. She turned her head slowly to listen as the wind calmed. It was as if the air was suddenly sucked out of their immediate area, leaving an eerie stillness behind. There was no sound and no movement. Even their breathing calmed down to an unnoticeable pace.

Like a fallen rock, their winged pursuer plunged to the ground in front of them, smashing through a grove of trees. Its thick talons snapping a trunk in half as it landed atop it. It bared its toothy maw with an intimidating roar as its giant leathery wings stretched out and flapped in a scary procession.

Its rider, however, remained silent. His clothes were torn and dirty. A full quiver of arrows slung across his back with the bow held tightly in his left hand. A rugged full beard and stringy matted hair gave him a savage appearance, keeping his face in heavy shadow. He stared intently at them through darkened eyes.

The unicorn let out a high-pitched whinny as it reared back on its hind legs while its front legs chopped at the wind, kicking toward the face of the lion, only annoying it. Settling back on the ground, the unicorn waited for the scary beast to react.

But before it could, Maxwell lunged for the creature's throat!

While much smaller than the beast's enormous head, Maxwell bit deep into its neck. With a mouthful of thick hair tufts, the dog was unable to do any real damage, the lion's hefty mane protecting it from harm. And shaking its head like a rag doll, it was able to dislodge the canine, hurling it into a broken tree stump.

"*NOOOOOO!*" shouted the wild girl. "Leave him alone!"

Maxwell was slow to get up, but get up he did, to let out a low growl to show he was all right.

Before the winged creature could turn its attention back on them, the unicorn spun its backside around, almost throwing its passengers off in the process. With a quick snap, its hind legs kicked the creature in the face with its stocky hooves. It made the creature more angry than hurt. It roared again, this time showing multiple rows of sharp teeth.

Without hesitation, its rider had already drawn an arrow from its quiver and aimed his bow toward the wild girl. At this close range, it was an easy shot to her head. With a quick release, he shot the projectile at her.

But it was snatched out of the air before it reached its intended target.

Maxwell landed on the ground after catching the sharpened stick in his mouth. He snapped it in his jaw, shattering it into pieces.

"Good boy!" cheered Esmeralda.

Before the rider could draw another arrow, the unicorn galloped away with Maxwell following close behind, trying to put as much distance between them and the creature.

The winged beast gave chase again, but it decided against a pursuit by air. This time, tucking its wings back and holding them close to its body to make itself more aerodynamic, it chased its victims by land. It was a choice decidedly slower, but more animalistic and savage in nature, as the predator pursued its prey. Its muscular paws pounded the ground as it sprinted after them.

Even though they had the lead, the unicorn was already slowing down. It had to weave between, around, and over all the obstacles in the forest, while the creature pursued in a straight and direct path. Its massive body able to plow through anything in its way. It exploded through rock formations and tore through trees, as its claws slashed through the underbrush, its horns lowered to ram through a briar patch.

The chase was short-lived. The unicorn had run itself into a dead end against a granite wall of impenetrable rock at the bottom of a valley. They could run no farther.

"We're stuck here. Go back!" said Atticus nervously.

"Just let me think," the wild girl told them.

Even Esmeralda was concerned. "But we can't stay here. It's going to be here any sec—"

And then it was. A long shadow cast down over them. At the top of the path, blocking their only way out, stood the creature.

The unicorn trotted around in circle. Its hooves scuffing the dirt with anxiety. The creature dug its claws into the ground, kneading it like bread. As the unicorn turned to face its pursuer, its nostrils flared and fumed. The creature let out a deep purr that sounded like gravel.

As it stalked toward them, its giant barbed

scorpion tail arced up in the air with a rigid stiffness. The razor-sharp prong at the end of it glistened in the light. Then the tail curled over the top of the rider, hanging over his head and pointing directly at them.

In a blink, its tail lashed out in attack.

The unicorn blinked back, shuffling to the side to avoid the strike. Then shuffling again the opposite direction. Each time, the tail whipped closer as the air crackled around them. And each time, the unicorn narrowly avoided it.

The creature pounced forward to allow its tail more room to thrust. Anticipating this, the unicorn knelt on its front knees to lower its body, and the sharp tail snapped over the tops of their heads, missing them.

With a new plan of attack, the creature reared back its tail as its sharpened tip began to glow.

"Everyone duck!" shouted the wild girl as she leaned forward to hug the neck of her steed. The twins also leaned forward to bow their heads out of the way.

A volley of green glowing liquid squirted toward them, flying above their shoulders and striking the granite wall behind them. The acid dissolved some of the rock as it melted away.

Before it could shoot again, the wild girl dismounted.

"What are you doing?" whispered Atticus. But she ignored him.

The twins watched in horror as the wild girl walked in front of her unicorn to face the rider and his beast. She held up her arms in a show of surrender. The wild girl offered her adversary a truce.

"I know what you want. And you can have it. As long as you don't hurt them," she said.

After a momentary pause for her words to sink in, the rider spoke for the first time. His voice was coarse but determined.

"Give it back. I make no promises."

"If that's how you want to play it," smirked the wild girl.

As if practiced on cue, she did a standing backflip to remount her unicorn. And, after giving the unicorn a quick kick in its side, it charged toward the beast. And the beast was unprepared.

The unicorn's singular horn struck into the shoulder of the creature, drilling through skin and muscle. It let out an anguished howl, and its talons scraped across the unicorn's hide. The horse continued past it as it barreled into the creature's wing, tearing a hole in its stretched, leathery skin. This caused it to topple onto its side, pinning the leg of its rider underneath its heavy body. The unicorn hurdled the scorpion tail as it whipped across the ground toward it, and didn't break stride as it raced away.

Esmeralda held tightly onto her brother as she looked behind them. The rider and creature were too injured to pursue. But she noticed an outstretched bow rise from behind the body of the creature, aimed into the air.

"Heads up!" shouted Esmeralda.

As they sprinted away, a few stray arrows harmlessly struck the ground behind them; they were long out of range. Their triumphant moment was thrilling enough to even make Atticus feel emboldened.

"Better luck next time!" Atticus shouted.

They came to a clearing and stopped. The man riding the creature wasn't following, or at least couldn't be seen. The twins wondered where they'd go to next.

The girl removed a gold pocket watch and dangled it by its chain. She wound its dial and stared at it intensely. What was so important about checking the time now of all things, Atticus wondered. The wild girl sensed they had their eyes on her, so she tried to ease their concern.

"Hold on. We're leaving," she assured them.

She began to spin the pocket watch in a clockwise pattern. It made a funny hum, quite similar to the obelisk itself. Sparks of electricity crackled in the air as it spun, generating a rectangular doorway in space. The watch swung to a stop, and the wild girl placed it safely back in her pocket. No sooner was it stuffed away that the unicorn charged toward the open doorway and jumped into it. Maxwell followed close behind.

The doorway of light closed around them as they phased through, disappearing into the ether.

CHAPTER 15

With a crackle of electrical energy and a sonic boom, they emerged from the pocket watch doorway into a new area. One they immediately grew to appreciate.

The cloudless lavender sky above them stretched across the horizon. The sound of a small bubbling brook cascaded down into a wide lake that sparkled across its still waters. Tall mountains formed along the perimeter. And they stood in the middle of rolling fields of orange grass. A calm breeze washed

across their faces, blowing through their hair. At this moment, they felt at peace.

The wild girl slid off the back of the unicorn as the twins also dismounted. The unicorn lowered its head toward her as they touched foreheads. She whispered some words of thanks as its ears rotated and twitched. The unicorn seemed to understand, nodding its head a few times, before it turned to leave them and trotted out to the orange fields to graze.

"Is it still hurt?" asked Esmeralda.

"Unicorns can heal quicker on their own. They have a fantastic healing ability. I just needed to remove the arrow to help it get started," answered the wild girl. "Don't worry. She'll be fine."

The wild girl started to walk in the opposite direction. She intended for the twins to follow her.

"We're almost home," she told them. "I mean my home. It's a short walk from here."

"Where are we?" asked Atticus.

"I don't believe there's a name for any of these places. None that I know," said the wild girl. "I never needed to call it anything to anyone. And never had anyone to tell it to. Until now."

They continued their walk over the hill and spotted their destination. A large hollowed out tree stump the size of a redwood was perched alone on this hill. A forest of fully grown trees was farther ahead in its backyard.

They stood before a crack in the wood at its base that was an entry point, without need for a door. In fact, there was no fencing or walls around the tree. Nothing to keep anyone out, which concerned Atticus, given the dangers they'd already faced.

"I can tell from your expression that you're worried," noticed the wild girl. "Don't be. At least not here. We're safe. Unlike other areas, there are no dangerous creatures where we are now. And no way for them to reach us."

"That's what we thought, until a Basilisk followed us from somewhere here, back to our school," said Atticus. Esmeralda reluctantly agreed.

"I'm sure you have a lot of questions," she surmised. "Are you hungry? Let's get inside and continue this talk over food."

They passed through the open entryway, ducking their heads as they entered. The first thing they noticed was that the hollowed out stump was entirely open from the top. There was no roof or covering to it, leaving them exposed.

"It doesn't rain here or get hot," explained the wild girl. "So I just left it that way. And you'll appreciate that when the night breeze blows through from the lake. It always puts me right to sleep."

"We don't plan to stay the night," Atticus told her.

"You'll find a lot of things here aren't for you to decide," said the wild girl.

The wild girl gathered a bowl filled with various fruits and nuts. Most looked familiar to the twins. But then some, with their strange purple and blue coloring or striped patterns, were like nothing they'd ever seen before.

"Go ahead, eat," she said. "I picked and gathered those from all the different areas I've traveled to. They're very fresh and taste great."

Esmeralda munched on something maroon in color, and green juice oozed out of it. She wiped her face with the back of her forearm.

"Mrlpfff . . . she's right . . . these are sweet," said Esmeralda with a mouthful, handing the half-eaten fruit to her brother.

"No thanks," he said, crossing his arms, either not hungry or just defiant.

The wild girl gathered sticks from a pile and placed them in a small pit. Striking a pair of stones together, she started a fire, and placed some fish on skewers over it to cook. The smoke began to rise out the top of her hollowed out tree home. Atticus couldn't help but think that the cooking fish smelled really good.

"I caught these over in the lake we passed. It makes things easier with food being so close," the wild girl said.

Esmeralda elbowed her brother, "Just like back home with our refrigerator as we work."

Maxwell was seated next to the wild girl as she cooked. She looked over at him and wiped a tear from her eye, and quickly wrapped her arms around him to give him a tight hug. She didn't want to let go.

"I still can't believe you're here, Maxwell! I've been looking for you forever!"

It finally dawned on Atticus. "You're Melanie! That was your Maxwell on your missing dog flyer."

The wild girl went back to spinning the fish over in the flames. "You saw that? That's been a while ago."

She removed the first fish and put it at Maxwell's feet. He barely sniffed it before guzzling it down. She carried two more fish over to her guests and handed it to them. This time, Atticus took it and began to chew.When he bit into it, it was fried on the outside and warmly soft on the inside. His sister smiled at him with full cheeks and he smiled back.

"I'm sure you've got like a million questions," the wild girl said. "But let me try to explain some things first.

"That pocket watch I used can open doors between dimensions. But only that giant clock you came through can take us all back home."

"Who was the man that attacked us?" asked Esmeralda.

"I don't know his real name, but I call him The Shepherd. I think he's been here even longer than I have. And the pocket watch was his. I took it from him the last time he tried to attack me. It's the only one he had; he said so himself. Either he built it or just owned it. But I worry he might make another."

"Why did you call him The Shepherd?" inquired Atticus.

"He seems to have dominance over the creatures throughout these dimensions," the wild girl replied. "And there are so many beasts here. But his favorite is that one he rides. The manticore. We've got to be careful around it with its claws and bite, the horns on its head, its wings that can fly, and especially that stinging tail. Its mouth alone has three rows of teeth!"

"Fascinating . . . but scary," whimpered Atticus.

"Those arrows he shot at us were created from the spines from its tail. The Shepherd is very crafty!" the wild girl observed.

"What's his problem? Why's he after us?" asked Esmeralda.

"You're the first people from the other side that he's seen in ages. Same with me," the wild girl said. "Which makes you the most important people here."

The wild girl stopped eating and rested her fish in her lap. She placed her hand on Maxwell's head and softly petted him. He leaned into her and closed his eyes.

"I'm sorry I yelled at you before, when we first met," the wild girl apologized. "But I am thankful you found me. But I also regret it."

Now Esmeralda stopped eating and seemed curious. "Why's that?"

"That clock in my house opens once to get here and once to leave, each time it's activated. I think it has something to do with turning the clock hands. And there's only a limited time before that doorway will reappear and then disappear. And once that happens, that's it."

Atticus swallowed the last of his fish hard. They never reset the clock hands when they came here this last time, trying to run from the Mordreds. They weren't even in the same area they entered from anymore. The wild girl realized it too.

Her next words were the most haunting.

"By now, the doorway back would've closed. You're now stuck here with me forever."

DEREK FRIDOLFS is the *New York Times* bestselling writer of the Secret Hero Society series at Scholastic and the Eisner-nominated co-writer of Batman Li'l Gotham at DC Comics. In his twenty-year career, he's written and drawn a range of comic book stories with *Scooby-Doo, Looney Tunes, Adventure Time, Teen Titans Go!, Wonder Woman, Superman,* and *Batman.* Also for one summer in middle school, he was tasked with house-sitting for a high school zoology teacher. Her family of pets included an antisocial garage cat, a tail-whipping iguana, some giant snapping macaws, and a cage full of panicked baby quail that got loose. Deciding animal care wasn't the career he wanted, his path to becoming a writer became clear. No animals were harmed in the making of this book (and all baby quail were recaptured by throwing a towel over them. They're very fast, you know!).

DUSTIN NGUYEN is a *New York Times* bestselling and Eisner Award–winning American comics creator. His body of work includes *Batman: Li'l Gotham*, which he cocreated, and numerous DC, Marvel, Dark Horse, and Boom! titles along with DC Comics Secret Hero Society and Image Comics' *Descender* and *Ascender*, both of which he cocreated. He lives in California with his wife, Nicole; their two kids, Bradley and Kaeli; and dog, Max. His first children's picture book, *What Is It?*, was written by his wife (at the age of ten) and is their first collaboration together. He enjoys sleeping and driving.

Lost on the other side with no
way back,

what are the Fetch Twins willing
to sacrifice

for a chance to return?

Find out in . . .

HALF PAST PECULIAR 2

COMING SOON . . .